The Fight for Justice

The Fight for Justice

JOHN PEEL

SCHOLASTIC INC.
New York Toronto London Auckland Sydney

Cover art by Maren

ISBN 0-590-18902-6

12 11 10 9 8 7 6 5 4 3 2 1   8 9/9 0 1 2 3/0

Printed in the U.S.A.   40
First Scholastic printing, July 1998

The Fight for Justice

. . . So don't just dream about applying for the Academy, make it come true! You can find a career in space: Exploration, Starfleet, or Merchant Service. If you have the right stuff to take on the universe, dispatch your application and join the ranks of the proud!

I'll admit it. I keep playing the Space Academy Recruitment tape. I have it memorized, but I still like to listen to it. Windy just caught me in the tech-dome playing it again — but so what? So what if I have dreams of joining the Imperial forces? Windy, Fixer, and Deak can laugh about it because they're happy as farmers, living day in and day out with nothing happening. But why should I be embarrassed for wanting more? For having dreams beyond moisture farming?

Windy says I should grow up. That I'm a farm boy, just like him. But I'm not. I don't have a farming bone in my body. I was made for action, for radical maneuvering in my T-16, for bold adventures and risk-taking.

That's why I took Windy with me through the eye of the Stone Needle today. I guess I needed to show him I'm not just a farm boy like him. And maybe it worked. He was scared. Squealing the whole way, like a baby Jawa. And me? I was loving every minute of it. What a thrill to steer that fast, that close to death. I could hear the buzz of metal as my speeder eased through that needle of stone. And to know I was going to beat Fixer through the bottleneck! Yes. The only thing missing was my best friend Biggs.

Biggs is the only one who understands. And now that he's at the Academy, there is really no one I can talk to about all this. I'm sick of my friends telling me the Academy is for suckers. That it's all about taking orders, wearing a fancy uniform, losing your identity — and probably your life.

I'm ready for the Academy and I'm as trained as I can be. I've had my T-16 for several years now, and I can fly it better than almost anyone around here. Of course, there's not much competition, especially since hotshot Biggs left for training. Tatooine is a pretty small place. Small and boring — no sane pilot would hang around here for long. So the Academy is really the only place for me. Maybe before I go, I can visit the spaceport at Mos Eisley. I'd love to check out some of those ships! I can just imagine all the planets they might be going to: Alderaan! Coruscant! Endor! But they're just names to me from a vid-encyclopedia. If I could just *see* them. . . .

Tonight I saw a space battle. At least I think it was a space battle. I saw flashes of light out of the corner of my eye. And when I looked through my electrobinoculars, I saw two ships firing at each other.

I dropped everything and hopped on my landspeeder. Forget chores! I had to find my friends — Fixer and Windy had to see this. A real battle in our system! Why couldn't *I* be up there fighting for justice with the Imperials?

When I found my friends, I was in for another surprise. Biggs was with them! Back from the Academy. I was so happy to see him, I forgot about the battle. And by the time I remembered and convinced everyone to take a look, the action was over. Nothing to see. Here I was making a big stink about two ships firing at each other, and the ships were just sitting there in orbit, hanging out like a couple of fat banthas. Nobody believed me. Windy, Fixer, Cammie, and Deak all thought I made it up. Like I'm so overeager to join the Space Academy, I'm starting to see stars — and battles! Well, they've got zip imagination. And that's fine for them. You don't need much imagination to farm. But they don't need to laugh at my expense.

And to be honest, I was a little hurt that Biggs didn't believe me, either. Biggs and I have been through a lot together. And just because he's at the Academy and I'm not doesn't mean I'm imagining stuff like a little kid. Those ships were not refueling or switching cargoes. And it *wasn't* the suns reflecting on metal. Those ray blasts were unmistakable. *Something* was going on in orbit tonight. I don't know what. And I'll probably never find out. But after seeing that action, I wish more than ever that I could find a way off Tatooine . . . for good.

I thought today would be the best day of my life. The beginning of something new. Something worthwhile. And definitely something other than moisture farming!

I don't want to live my life on a constant quest for water. All we do here is fight against the hot, dry conditions of Tatooine. It takes all our efforts, running the vaporators full-time to produce enough water for survival.

Oh, Uncle Owen and Aunt Beru do okay. With my help, of course. But today I'm old enough to leave. And Uncle Owen *promised*.

Only he's gone back on that promise.

He says I have to work here for another year, and then he'll be able to spare me. I've worked here all my life. I thought I was getting the chance to stop wasting my time on this farm — and do something.

I know I shouldn't sound so harsh. I mean, Uncle Owen and Aunt Beru took me in when I was a baby, and they've raised me as if I were their own child. They never had any children themselves, and they've always been good to me. I don't have any complaints there, although I would have liked to have known my parents.

And this farm is Uncle Owen's life. He's a good man, I know that. But his horizons stretch only as far as the farm does. He rarely goes to town anymore, preferring to send me on errands for him. He stays out here, working and sweating all day to produce a little moisture. And he's happy with that. It's a tiring life, but the one he chooses.

The problem is that I can't make him see it's not the life *I* choose. The thought of spending my life here, rejigging failing vaporators and programming farm droids, makes me want to scream. I want to experience life out in the galaxy — where things really happen! Sometimes, I just sit out at night, looking up at the stars, and imagine what it would be like to be out there.

Of course, Biggs doesn't have to imagine anymore. He's graduated from the Academy already, and has earned his wings. I'm really glad for him, but I'd be lying if I said I wasn't jealous, too. He's going to be out there in space, flying and visiting all the places we've talked about a hundred times.

It was so great to see Biggs. But it made me realize how much I miss him. And that I'll have another full year without a best friend to fly T-16s with. He's already way ahead of me, but he didn't rub it in, and told me kind of casually, like it wasn't any big deal. But I could see the pride in his eyes, and hear the hunger in his voice.

Thankfully, I can encode these entries so nobody else can play them back. Otherwise, I'd never be revealing what Biggs told me. He isn't planning to stick with his job on a freighter. He's going to jump ship at the first port of call, and join the Rebellion!

I told him he was crazy to think he could actually find the Rebels. I mean, if the Empire can't find them, what are *his* chances? And even if he does find them, I'm not so sure that's such a great thing. I mean, we all know that the current government isn't the greatest in the galaxy. They take their cut of everything, and they supposedly enforce the peace. But, on the whole, they pretty much leave Tatooine alone.

Not that there's anything here to interest them anyway.

Sure I've heard about some terrible things the Emperor's troops have done. But they're just stories. I've never met anyone who could actually back up the stories with facts. It might be nothing more than discontented grumblings. Then again, maybe the stories are all true, and the Emperor's the tyrant they claim, and he deserves to be overthrown. I don't know. It's just politics as usual. It has nothing to do with me.

Of course, if I were out there among the stars, maybe I'd know more. Then I could make a decision — even the same one Biggs has made. He definitely believes he's doing the right thing. And knowing Biggs, he probably is.

I guess Biggs worries about me as much as I worry about him. He tried to talk me into leaving the farm. He said I needed to think about what's important in life. Get my priorities straight. He knows why I've worked so hard at becoming the hottest, fastest, most daring pilot in town. But going off and doing what he did . . . it's just not that easy.

Uncle Owen won't let me leave, and I owe him and Aunt Beru too much just to walk out on them. At first, I thought Uncle Owen didn't want to let me go because I'm cheap help around the farm. But it's more than that. He seems *afraid*. Like he knows that if I had the chance, I'd kick the dust of this planet off my feet and never come back. And he's afraid of what might happen to me if I do that.

But can't he see what will happen to me if I *don't*? This planet will suck all the life out of me. My body would walk around doing chores, but my spirit would be dead. I don't know how I'll ever do it, but someday, I have to get out of here — out among the stars. There are so many worlds and wonders to see, so much to discover.

It's where I'm meant to be. I know it is.

My day started with a visit from the Jawa traders. Uncle Owen wanted a couple of extra droids to help out on the farm, and the Jawas are pretty good at scavenging used droids. Of course, you have to know what you're doing when you buy from them. They'll assure you that everything's first-class merchandise, then sell you a piece of scrap that keeps going just long enough for them to get out of the area.

But Uncle Owen's pretty good at spotting those kinds of deals. He can bargain the Jawas down without any problem. And, while I'm by no means a master mechanic, I can usually tell quality merchandise when I see it.

The Jawa sandcrawler stopped by, as they do from time to time. Those things are huge, slow, and noisy, so you have plenty of warning before they arrive. The Jawas live and work in them, so they're kind of like a small town on wheels. The smell inside the sandcrawler gets pretty bad, since Jawas aren't the cleanest of creatures. That's why they always line up whatever droids they've got to sell in the open air.

Uncle Owen looked the lineup over and picked out a protocol droid and a handy little R2-5 unit. But the R2-5 blew its motivator, so Uncle Owen went for a different R2 unit instead. The interpreter — his name is See-Threepio — and Artoo-Deetoo know each other, that's apparent. They spend a lot of time bickering and blaming one another for everything, but they both seem like good little units.

Only I think Artoo must have a few loose bolts. He claims he belongs to an Obi-Wan Kenobi.

Kenobi's a fine name, but there's nobody around here named Obi-Wan. The only Kenobi I've ever heard of is an old guy named Ben. He's kind of . . . eccentric. He's lived on his own in the Dune Sea for as long as I can remember. I've only met him once, about five seasons back.

Windy and I had been out in Beggar's Canyon. We were lost, and it got a bit hairy for a while, but Ben Kenobi arrived to help us. It was kind of odd that he just showed up out of the blue like that. But we were just happy he could guide us back to the farm.

The odd thing is, Uncle Owen really hates the old guy for some reason. He lit into Ben, accusing him of all kinds of stuff, instead of thanking him for helping us get home. Then he told Ben to get out and never come back.

Before Ben left, he gave me an odd kind of look, like he was committing me to memory for some future date.

Then Uncle Owen wanted to know everything Ben had said. I really didn't remember much, and most of what I could recall didn't make much sense. Ben seemed a bit like a fanatic. Harmless, but really into his beliefs. Uncle Owen told me that Ben's a little crazy from living alone and being out in the sun too much.

Anyway, Ben's the only Kenobi I know, and he certainly never owned any droids. He doesn't like mechanical things. I've even heard he *walks* everywhere!

Artoo was telling the truth about there being an Obi-Wan, though. I was giving him a quick cleaning, to get the grime from the sandcrawler off him, when I accidentally triggered a recording.

He projected a short holographic message. It didn't make much sense, but I've already memorized it. It was from one of the most beautiful girls I've ever seen in my life. Not that I've seen too many girls — there aren't many out here on the moisture farms. But this one in the projection just took my breath away! I know I'm probably crazy, but there's just something about her. I feel like I've known her all of my life.

It feels as if she's a part of me somehow.

Whoever she is, she's obviously highborn. Her accent gives that away. I know she's not the kind of girl I would ever get to know, but I can't help wishing for someone like her.

And she's in trouble, too. The message repeated, over and over. "Help me, Obi-Wan Kenobi . . . you're my only hope." Whoever this Obi-Wan Kenobi is, I wish I could find him, and pass the message on. This girl might still be in serious trouble, and maybe I'm the only one who can help her.

Ah, who am I kidding?

I took off Artoo's restraining bolt, in hopes of releasing more of the message, but instead the message vanished. Artoo couldn't bring it back up, so it's probably really old. Both of the droids are pretty battered up, and they've seen some action. See-Threepio said he thinks the girl was a passenger on his last ship, but the recording was probably made before he even met Artoo. It could be a couple of decades old, even. I'll bet the girl is middle-aged, married, and raising a bunch of kids.

Ahhh, I really should quit my dreaming and accept that nothing interesting is ever going to happen to me.

So much has happened since yesterday, I don't know if I'll ever get my thoughts straight. I wish I had someone to talk to, to help me figure all this stuff out.

I'm in a small cabin on the starship *Millennium Falcon*, and I'm being hunted by stormtroopers. It's still hard to grasp that this is really happening to me.

I really underestimated that little R2 unit. Sometimes I forget how smart droids can be. Artoo sure pulled a fast one on me last night. He didn't need the restraining bolt pulled to free up that message of his at all. He needed it pulled so that he could *escape*.

He left last night, but it was too dangerous then to look for him.

See-Threepio had remained behind; he still had *his* restraining bolt. But Artoo had his mechanical mind fixated on Obi-Wan Kenobi, and he must have had some kind of directions as to where to find him, because he'd set off alone, at night, across the Dune Sea.

I was even more certain than before that he had to be malfunctioning. Nobody in his right mind, human or droid, would go there. For one thing, the temperatures get *really* high. A human can dehydrate in about thirty minutes. Droids don't dehydrate, but the sun and sand can be dangerous. All that metal attracts the heat, overloading their cooling systems, and, no matter how careful you are, sand gets into everything. It can really ruin a droid's insides.

And then there are the Sand People, otherwise known as Tusken Raiders. They don't come around much, but when they do, nothing and nobody is safe from them.

I didn't have much choice but to go after him. Not so much for Artoo's sake — though I did feel kind of sorry for the small droid — but because we really needed him to help with the harvest. I didn't dare tell Uncle Owen what the droid had done. He'd just have a fit and probably decide to scrap him and make me do his work instead.

So there was nothing to do but load up my landspeeder and head off after him. If the winds hadn't been too brisk, I knew I could follow his trail. Threepio talked me into letting him come along, claiming he could reason with the

R2 unit. He hadn't been too good at that so far, but if he came along, then it meant I'd be able to keep an eye on him, too. He claims to be loyal, but so did Artoo — right before he took off.

We picked up some of Artoo's trail, heading straight for the Jundland Wastes. That was interesting, because that was the direction Ben Kenobi lived in. It was also where the Sand People were rumored to be hanging out.

I'd brought my blaster pistol along, just in case. I'm a pretty good shot with it, if I do say so myself. But I've never shot anything bigger than a womp rat, and they're not exactly bright. Vicious, yes, but pretty dumb, too. I wasn't sure I could bring myself to kill a Sand Person, though. They may be savages, but they're intelligent beings.

Even shooting one in self-defense would make me feel funny.

Not that I got the chance. We headed out and finally picked up Artoo. He was trundling along a canyon, still headed for the Dune Sea. I ordered him to stop, but he refused. He kept carrying on about his mission, the secret plans, and having to get to Obi-Wan Kenobi. I have to admit, I thought he was just overheating. And what an imagination! All that stuff about a secret mission was unbelievable.

But things went from bad to worse. Artoo detected something, so I checked it out with my electrobinoculars. I caught sight of a couple of banthas, being watched by a Sand Person. At first, I didn't get it. They always rode one to a bantha. Why was there only one Sand Person, with *two* banthas, then?

Simple. The other Sand Person was stalking me!

But before I could figure this out, it attacked me, knocking me down. I didn't even get a chance to use my blaster.

Sand People are really tall and built like steel walls. This one knocked Threepio over a short drop and slammed me into the ground.

Then it came at me with its gaderffii stick.

Staring right into the face of death does something to you. I mean, I had never really thought about dying before. I always knew it happened to everyone eventually, but not to me, not *now.* Even the crazy flying races I've done with Biggs and Windy were more like games than something that could kill you. But I saw in the way it attacked that it was going to kill me. It raised its weapon.

And I was too stunned to fight back.

I thought I was doomed. That this was the end. I'd never get to explore the galaxy. Never see the stars up close, or visit any other worlds. I couldn't believe I was going to be killed for the contents of my landspeeder and a couple of droids.

It seemed so futile, so pointless, dying out there like that.

And then there came this really strange noise — it took me a couple of seconds to recognize it as a krayt dragon. It howled and echoed all over the place, sending tingles up my spine. It did worse than that to the Sand Person, though. I couldn't see his face, of course — but every muscle in his body spelled *fear.* The next thing I knew, the Tusken Raider was gone.

First of all, I was *really* glad to be alive. I knew how lucky I was. And second, I was getting really scared, lying there on the ground as the creature that scared the Tusken Raider approached me. But I simply didn't have the strength to get up and flee for safety. I'd banged my head pretty badly when I fell, and I couldn't get to my feet.

Then the monster appeared.

If I hadn't been so shaken, I might have laughed. The *monster* turned out to be an old man in protective robes, carrying something like a horn, through which he blew to produce that terrible shriek. It was old Ben Kenobi, and he'd managed to save my life a second time!

His fingers obviously had some skill, because

he managed to help me to my feet by manipulating my aching muscles and nerves. That and a sip of water had me feeling better in a couple of minutes.

It turned out that Ben had imitated the cry of a krayt dragon, the one thing that terrifies the Sand People, which is why they'd fled without looking back. He might be an eccentric old hermit, as Uncle Owen said, but he was certainly good at arriving just when he was needed — and at knowing exactly what to do.

I didn't see how this could have been pure co-incidence, Ben finding me. But it made more sense to believe Ben was just passing by, than to believe he somehow sensed my trouble.

But that's the weird thing — Ben *had* been looking for me.

He was surprised to discover I was with a couple of droids, though. Even more so when he discovered that Artoo claimed to belong to him.

You see, Ben *is* Obi-Wan Kenobi. I'm not sure what it's all about, except that he used to be somebody really important — a Jedi Knight. And then, for some reason, he decided to lay low for a while. So he started calling himself Ben Kenobi instead. It seems kind of odd to me, but I soon discovered that Ben wasn't as crazy as Uncle Owen tried to make him sound. A bit eccentric, maybe, but not crazy.

Ben took us to his house. Threepio was damaged by the Tusken Raider attack, and I needed to do some quick repairs. I couldn't take him back to the farm in the state he was in. My uncle would have been furious.

His house was small and simple. He had a few gadgets, like a vaporator to get his own water and stuff like that. But there were no droids or any sort of transportation. He really *did* walk everywhere!

I don't think I could do without droids or speeders or any of a hundred other things, but Ben doesn't need them and doesn't miss them.

I could hardly believe it when he told me he was a Jedi Knight. I mean, I didn't know there were any Jedi Knights left. I wasn't even sure they'd ever existed in the past.

When I was young, I'd heard about the Jedi from someone at school. I asked my uncle Owen about them, and he told me that they were just stories. Aunt Beru had told me that there *were* once great and wise knights who kept the peace, called Jedi, but that they were long gone. "Most of the stories they tell about them just grew and grew," she explained. "Don't believe everything you hear."

And here was Ben, telling me that he'd been a Jedi Knight in his youth! It was incredible, partly to discover that there really had been

Jedi, and partly because "crazy old Ben" had been one of them.

And then Ben really surprised me. He told me that my *father* had also been a Jedi — and his close friend!

My father . . .

All my life, I've wondered about my father. What kind of a man was he? Uncle Owen had never told me much, just that he had been a navigator on a spice freighter. It takes skill to pilot your way around hyperspace, and I always figured I had inherited my piloting skills from my father. Uncle Owen had never told me that my father was also a Jedi.

According to Ben, my father was a hero — a great pilot, a great warrior, and a great man. He had been trained by Ben to become a Jedi, and my father was one of Ben's best pupils.

Uncle Owen knew all about this, too, but he'd never revealed a word of it to me. Ben thinks Uncle Owen was wrong to hide the truth, but he won't come right out and say so.

I can see that Uncle Owen really believed what he was doing was right. He stopped me from ever learning how to fight, and from learning the truth about my father. He tried to make me like he was: a farmer, not an adventurer.

But that was *him*, not *me*. I guess that, even

though I never knew them, there's a lot of my parents in me. That's why I've always been so restless, always looking for something more. I knew I was missing something, only I never understood what it was. Now I think I'm starting to.

Apparently that fight my Uncle Owen had with Ben was because Ben wanted to tell me the truth, and Uncle Owen wouldn't allow it. That's why he threw Ben out and asked me all those questions about what Ben had been telling me.

It turns out that Ben's been keeping an eye on me in his own way. That's how he knew I was in trouble today and showed up just in time to help me.

And then he offered me a gift, something that had belonged to my father. It didn't look like much, just a small, stocky rod with a button it. But it was my father's lightsaber.

A lightsaber!

I'd heard of such weapons, but I'd never seen one. According to the stories, a Jedi was given his lightsaber on his first day of training. Ben told me that it requires great skill to use a lightsaber, unlike a blaster or a fusion cutter. That's why it was considered a great symbol to be able to use it *well*. And Ben said my father wanted me to have it when I was old enough.

Ben actually wanted to give it to me when we'd met five seasons ago, but Uncle Owen had flatly refused. He was afraid that if I held a lightsaber, I'd go off on some mad crusade with Ben.

Maybe he was right to be worried. Just holding the lightsaber in my hand, and making slow, careful moves with it, felt . . . I don't know. Like nothing I'd ever felt before. It felt as if it were a part of me; I was somehow connected to it. Not like a blaster — that's just a weapon you pick up and shoot. The lightsaber is something elegant, controlled . . . it just feels so *right* when I hold it in my hand.

And it had been my father's. I could almost feel him there, as if his hand, too, were still holding it. I was linked across time to my father through that lightsaber, and it felt good.

I'll tell you one thing: I'm never letting my lightsaber go.

SIXTH ENTRY

I finally worked up the courage to ask Ben about my father's death. Uncle Owen had never talked about it, simply saying that he'd died during the war. I was sure that Ben knew more than that, and I was right. He told me that it was a complicated story, but that it involved another of his pupils, a man named Darth Vader.

Vader, he told me, was once a Jedi, one of the greatest ever. But he'd become corrupt and now serves the Emperor. Vader had hunted down and killed all the Jedi Knights in the galaxy. Only he obviously missed a few, since Obi-Wan was still alive.

All of this made me think. If the man who killed my father is loyal to the Empire, it must mean that my father would have fought against the Empire if he were still alive.

How can I sit on the sidelines, then, while the Rebellion rages on, if my father would not?

Ben tried to explain to me what it means to be a Jedi. It's something to do with what Ben calls the Force. I'm not sure I really understand this yet, but he says I will with time. Ben says the Force is something that is in each and every atom in the universe. It's not a physical force, like gravity or magnetism, but a Force that links everything together. It sounds like some sort of religion to me, but Ben insists that it's not.

Anyway, because this Force is everywhere, it means that if you have the potential to use the Force you can do all kinds of things that normal people can't do. It's not magic, it's just making use of the Force. Ben says he'll teach me all about it, so maybe I'll understand it better later. Right now, I'm mostly confused.

But I do understand one thing: Darth Vader deliberately misuses the Force. Ben says there's a dark side to it, one that enables a Jedi to use it for selfish purposes, and for evil. Vader is a master of the dark side of the Force, while Ben works only with the good.

I know now that there is one thing I must do: I have to find Darth Vader and make him pay for what he did to my father.

I know, it sounds crazy, but he can't be allowed to get away with everything he's done. I swear here and now that I'm going to find him and settle this debt.

Suddenly Ben stopped telling me about Vader and the Force because Artoo was so insistent that Ben pay attention to him. After everything I'd been through, I'd forgotten all about the girl's call for help.

Last night I'd managed to convince myself that the message was old and nothing to worry about. But Artoo still insisted it was urgent.

Despite the fact that Ben doesn't keep any droids, it was obvious that he was pretty familiar with them. He tinkered with Artoo for a couple of minutes and got the message up and running.

This time it was the whole message. The same beautiful girl, this time telling Obi-Wan Kenobi that she'd gotten hold of some vital plans from the Empire, and that they were urgently needed on Alderaan, where her father would know what to do with them. She begged for his help, which was the bit of the message I'd caught last night.

I was wrong about it being ancient history. It seems that the message was recorded only days ago. We got most of the story from Threepio, who was amazed by the message. Apparently he hadn't seen the girl give the message to Artoo.

It turns out that the two droids were on one of the two ships I'd seen fighting. The ones my friends thought I had imagined!

It was some sort of official ship from Alder-aan, and it had been attacked by an Imperial Cruiser. Artoo had vanished for a bit during the fighting, which was when he'd been given the message.

Then he'd taken Threepio into an escape pod and they were ejected. They'd landed on Tatooine and started out for Ben's place, but had been captured by Jawas and sold to Uncle Owen.

As soon as the hologram message ended, it was obvious that Ben planned to do something about it. I could see the change come over him. One minute he was cordial and cheerful, talking to me about my father. The next he was grim and intent.

"Who was that girl?" I asked him. If she was real, and still looked like that, then I really wanted to meet her.

Ben told me she is Princess Leia Organa of the planet Alderaan, and that she's an Imperial Senator.

Ouch! Talk about being out of my league! A princess? Well, that figures. She was so beau-tiful and so commanding, she'd have to be a princess. And a politician, too. And here I am thinking I might stand a chance with her!

Maybe it is impossible, but I'd like nothing more than to meet her someday. Especially if I'm going to be a Jedi Knight. Maybe as a Jedi

I can dedicate myself to guarding a lady. I can do that for her. Maybe she'd never even notice me, but that doesn't mean I can't protect her.

But I'm getting ahead of myself, talking about being a Jedi. That was the last thing on my mind right then. Well, okay, not the *last* thing. My father had been a Jedi, and the idea of following in his footsteps was really exciting. Plus, Ben was definitely encouraging the idea! Now that he'd heard the message, he wanted to set off for Alderaan, just like that — and he wanted me to go with him!

He didn't know how tempting that was! To be off on a quest, my father's lightsaber in my hand, some beautiful princess to save . . . if only I could! But that was a mission for a dreamer, for a poet, for a crazy old man like Ben Kenobi. I wasn't any of those things. My uncle Owen depended on me to get the crops to grow on his farm. I had to think about my responsibilities.

And since I've promised myself to tell the truth on this record, I'll admit my fears.

Maybe my father had been a Jedi, but that didn't mean I could be. I'm not the most skillful person in the world, though I'm a pretty great pilot. What if I turned out to be a lousy Jedi? Wouldn't that be worse than never trying?

Trying and failing . . . I couldn't face that.

At least on Tatooine I could have my dreams.

But what if trying to make them come true only showed me my failures? Could I stand that?

So when Ben told me that he wanted me to go with him, I couldn't do it. I tried to explain that I couldn't just up and leave my aunt and uncle like that. That it was the middle of the season, and they needed my help. That I'd been gone long enough as it was to get into trouble with my uncle. Ben looked at me calmly and let all of these excuses wash right over him. "That's your uncle talking," was his reply. I guess he was right, too. It *was* Uncle Owen, and not me.

In spite of my fears, I'd have loved to have gone with him, but it was just so *crazy*. I mean, romantic quests are fine, but we have to live our real lives, not some incredible adventures we dream up.

I could rationalize it in all kinds of ways. Ben was known to be a little touched in the head; I'd have to be just as crazy to go with him. I didn't really know him, after all. True, he'd saved my life twice, but I'd hardly spent any time with him.

But that was *logic* speaking, and logic isn't always enough. The funny thing is, from the moment I met Ben, I felt tied to him somehow. Sort of like fate, or destiny. Or maybe it's that Force he's always talking about. The point is, I feel as if I've known Ben all of my life. So when he said, "We're off to Alderaan," it didn't seem that odd. Just impossible, because I'd never get my chores done.

To my surprise, Ben didn't try to talk me out of it. I was expecting him to try his best, but that's obviously not Ben's way. When you've made a decision and told him, he won't argue with you, even if he thinks you're wrong. He just nodded and said that I had to make up my own mind, and the Force within me would show me the right way to go.

I wish I knew what he was talking about. I don't feel any Force within me. Just a lot of confusing emotions and thoughts, all tugging me in different directions. I didn't know which ones I should be paying the most attention to. That was the problem. Ben and this Princess Leia needed help, and Ben seemed to have confidence that somehow I could be that help. But Uncle Owen needed my help, too. Shouldn't family come first? Or was that just my fears talking?

In the end, it didn't matter what I decided. Maybe Ben's right about the Force leading us in the right direction.

I offered to take Ben to Anchorhead, where he could get other transportation. He'd have to head over to Mos Eisley, the spaceport, to grab a ship to Alderaan. I couldn't take him that far; Uncle Owen would never let me hear the end of it. Ben accepted the offer, and we set off.

We never made it.

On the way, we saw smoke . . . and that meant trouble. Out here in the Dune Sea there's nothing to burn — no vegetation, at any rate. So if there was smoke, it had something to do with intelligent beings. Neither Ben nor I had a clue as to what the smoke was from, but it was clearly our duty to take a look and see if we could help.

We couldn't.

The smoke turned out to be a blazing sand-crawler. Somebody had blasted it apart and shot all of the Jawas. There were tiny bodies everywhere and the stench of scorched meat. It wouldn't be long before the womp rats would be around, looking to eat.

Threepio recognized the Jawas as the ones who had captured him and Artoo. I couldn't be sure myself, but he remembered plenty of details about the crawler and the other droids. Strangely enough, the droids had all been violently disassembled. I looked around and saw bantha tracks all over. There were even a couple of broken gaderffii sticks that the Sand People use.

It didn't make much sense to me. I know the Tusken Raiders are violent, and they're greedy. So why did they destroy the droids instead of taking them along as loot? I couldn't figure it out.

But Ben could. He pointed out the bantha tracks. Like I said, there were lots of them, and that's not something the Sand People do. Instead, they ride single file, so you can't tell how many of them there are. And then Ben pointed out the precision of the damage to the sandcrawler. Tuskens are kind of wild, and attack and shoot at anything. But the attackers here had been very careful and precise, first stopping and then demolishing the crawler. It wasn't Raider-style fighting, it was stormtrooper style.

Imperial stormtroopers!

Ben asked Threepio and Artoo to start gathering fuel and bodies for a pyre. He didn't want to leave the poor Jawas to be eaten by womp rats. I could sympathize with that; I've seen what womp rats do to carcasses and it isn't something I'd wish on any creature — even if they were dead.

As we started work, my mind was churning. Why had Imperials attacked the Jawas? Oh, Jawas are nuisances, and sometimes steal things, but nobody really minds them. Sometimes the authorities will clamp down a bit and throw a couple into jail. But to burn them out like this? It didn't make sense.

And then, all of a sudden, it started to.

These were the same Jawas who had captured the droids. And Artoo had plans inside him for something that would help the Rebellion. The stormtroopers must know that, and be looking for the two droids. They'd tracked them to the Jawas, and the Jawas didn't have them . . .

They'd be after whoever they thought had the droids now . . .

With a cry, I ran for the landspeeder. Nothing else mattered right then except to get home and warn my aunt and uncle.

It was a foolish thing to do, I know. Now I can see how dumb I was. Shooting right back to the farm while Imperials might be raiding it! And all I was armed with was my blaster and a lightsaber I didn't even know how to use!

But that didn't matter. What *did* matter was that the Imperials were going to be going after my aunt and uncle next. Some of the Jawas looked as if they'd survived the attack for a while. They had burn marks on their feet — a tell-tale sign they'd been made to talk.

I saw the smoke a long time before I saw the burning house. But it didn't take me long to find what was left of Uncle Owen and Aunt Beru.

I'm going to have to take another break. I can't talk about it right now. My aunt and uncle were the only family I had. And the Imperials murdered them both.

I'm feeling a little better now. But only a little.

It's really hard, still, to accept the fact that my aunt and uncle are dead.

The stormtroopers killed them and burned the house down to the ground. They made it look like Tusken Raiders again, but it was an even flimsier cover job this time. It just isn't like Sand People to attack a homestead. They don't like enclosed spaces so they stay away from small buildings. Nobody except a stupid stormtrooper would think they'd do such a thing.

It's hard not to feel like I failed them when they most needed me. If I'd been there, maybe I could have done something.

Of course, I might have been killed, too.

Ben says my survival is an example of the Force at work. He says the fact that I was not killed was not accidental. But rather, a miracle of the Force. That somehow, some cosmic Force was able to guide me out of harm's way. He says I'm very strong in the Force, but untrained.

He's started me on some exercises, ones he used to do with his students. It's hard to get the hang of it, but every now and then I really feel like I'm starting to understand the Force — and Obi-Wan Kenobi.

I've been thinking a lot about my aunt and uncle.

Maybe I'd had my disagreements with Uncle Owen, but I never doubted that he and Aunt Beru loved me. They'd always treated me like I was their own son. I remember one time — I must have been about six or seven — one of my friends teased me about not having a *real* father and mother. And Uncle Owen had said, proudly: "He *does* have a real father and mother. Nobody could love their boy more." And that made me feel pretty good.

They were always like that. I remember Aunt Beru taking care of me when I had the dust fever. She stayed with me for days, cooling me down, feeding me even when I didn't want to eat. It was like she was *willing* the fever to go down.

And now they would never do anything for

me again. But I could do one last thing for them.

My purpose became clear: Darth Vader was an Imperial, a servant of the Emperor, and the murderer of my father. Other Imperials had just killed what was left of my family. If the Empire could declare war on the Skywalkers, then it was time for the last Skywalker to fight back.

Ben was all I had left now, the last link to my past, my father — and to my future.

Even amid all the tears and rage I felt as I stood by the graves, I also felt an odd sort of peace. Like seeking an end to this kind of violence was the *right* thing to do. Ben says that I felt the stirring of the Force then, and I hope he's right. Because, for the first time in my life, I was absolutely certain of what to do.

I was going to help Ben, join the Rebellion, and overthrow the Empire! I was going to make Darth Vader and the Emperor sorry for what they had done. And, with a little luck, I was going to romance a princess. . . .

Right.

But we all need dreams to inspire us, and they inspired me. I managed to wipe away the tears and let my anger simmer down as I drove the landspeeder back to Ben. He and the droids had started the funeral pyre, and more Imperial victims were being burned. There had been a lot of deaths, and it was time someone started to pay for it.

Ben knew what had happened before I told him. He also knew I'd been an idiot to go off alone like that. But he didn't rub it in. He just waited, a terribly sad expression on his face. I told him what had happened, and how I should have been there to help Uncle Owen and Aunt Beru.

Ben pointed out that I'd only have been killed, too. I knew that, but it didn't alter the fact that I felt as if I'd left them to die.

I know here was no way I could have known in advance that the Imperials would go after my family. Until we'd heard that message in Ben's house, none of us had a clue as to what was going on.

Actually, we still don't. All we know is that Princess Leia Organa managed to put some-thing inside Artoo that the Empire wants very badly. We don't know what it is. Bail Organa on Alderaan will be able to get the information out and use it. All Ben and I have to do is see that the droid gets there safely. Then, maybe, we'll find out what all of this is about.

Anyway, I told Ben some of this, and he nod-ded. He was glad I'd agreed to come along with him. I got the impression that he'd known, somehow, that I would. He told me how sorry he was, but that he was ready to teach me how to become a Jedi Knight, just like my father.

My father . . . I'm sitting here, holding his lightsaber. Ben's been showing me how to hold it and use it. I'm starting to get the hang of it now, but I know I'll need to get a lot better before I can actually use it in battle. It'll be safer for me to stick with my blaster for the time being.

Ben isn't telling me everything he knows about my father. And to tell the truth, it's making me a little mad. I mean, he knew Anakin Skywalker for years, so he knows a lot. Most of it probably isn't very interesting to him, but it's stuff I'd love to know. Like, how did my father laugh? Was he always serious, or did he play jokes on people? What was most important to him? What did he like to eat for breakfast? Who were his other friends? Ben doesn't understand why I want to know this stuff, I can tell.

And there's something else, too. He was very . . . evasive . . . about how my father died. He only says that Darth Vader killed him. But he won't say how. And, most important, he didn't tell me where my parents are buried. I know it's probably pointless, but I'd really like to visit their graves. I didn't know them when they were alive, but maybe I'll learn something just seeing how and where they're buried.

Anyway, we set out together for Mos Eisley. I had nothing to hang around for. Almost everything I owned had been destroyed with my uncle's house. All I had left was the landspeeder, the droids, the clothes I wore, my blaster, and my father's lightsaber. Plus a few coins in my pockets. It wasn't much, but it was something, at least.

I'd never seen Mos Eisley before. Actually, I'd never seen any place bigger than Anchorhead, and that's only about twenty buildings. Mos Eisley was *huge*. There had to be thousands of buildings, and at the far edge was the spaceport, like a small city of its own. Ben had been here before, of course, so he knew what to do and where to go.

There were people and creatures everywhere. Species I'd never heard of before. Of course, I've seen aliens before. But not very many. There wasn't any reason for them to swing past Anchorhead, so few of them ever did. Mos Eisley was filled with all sorts of strange characters — strange-looking, strange-talking, and strange-smelling.

I'm sure a lot of them felt the same way about me, too!

Ben saw me staring and obviously knew how

I felt. He smiled and told me that Mos Eisley was one of the most depraved places in the galaxy. I could believe it. Most of the people and aliens looked very tough, and Ben told me that the port was rife with smugglers, thieves, and con men of all kinds.

It was also full of stormtroopers.

I'd never seen so many in one place before. There were *hundreds* of them, and they were checking everyone and everything. Once, I'd thought they looked invincible in their white armor; now, I was hoping I'd been wrong. Because these troopers were looking at me. And I'd seen what they did to people who got in their way. I started getting nervous and looked for a way out.

Ben calmed me down a little, explaining that it would attract attention if we tried to flee. Instead, he had me drive up to the closest checkpoint. I'll admit, I was nervous as anything, pulling up next to the troopers, with their blasters set and ready. The men eyed Artoo and Threepio and wanted to know how long I'd had them. I was sure the troopers could sense my fear.

"Two or three seasons," I lied, hoping Ben knew what he was doing.

Sweat was trickling down my back. I wanted to shudder, but did my best to look confused and casual. The troopers told us they were looking for stolen droids — which was obviously the story they'd dreamed up to explain what they were doing — and wanted to see my papers.

I did have papers, of course. Only there was a problem. They'd been burned in the house with my uncle and aunt.

Then Ben leaned forward. Staring directly at the stormtroopers, he told them in a low, intense voice that they didn't need to see our papers.

Then the weirdest thing happened.

The troopers repeated what Ben said, and when Ben said we could move on, they acted like it was their idea and waved us forward.

I got us moving as fast as I could, but my mind was whirling. I had *no* idea what had just happened. Ben explained that I had witnessed the power of the Force. It can affect certain minds, he told me — weak minds — if you're trained and they're not. But it wouldn't work on everyone, and it wouldn't last forever. So we had to hurry.

Ben had me drive to a cantina he knew of. I didn't ask how he knew about this place, but it obviously wasn't the sort of establishment he ever hung around himself. It was seedy, filled with low-life types, and reeked of alcohol and low-grade motor oil. There was an alien band playing in the corner, and a bartender with an attitude problem the size of an asteroid.

The bartender was prejudiced against droids, and flatly refused to allow us in unless we left Threepio and Artoo outside. I'd heard of people being like that; I guess they're bothered by the fact that droids are intelligent but artificial. I don't understand the attitude myself, but some people get really defensive about droids.

Ben had me leave them outside to avoid any trouble. I was worried that something might happen to the droids in this town. Droid thefts aren't unknown in the best of places, and this was far from the best of places.

It wasn't just that we *had* to get Artoo to Alderaan. To be honest, I was getting kind of attached to the two droids. Threepio is a bit . . . I almost said *stiff-necked*, but that's a given! He chatters on and on to the point where I have to shut him down to get any peace and quiet! But he has a good heart — or servo, or motivator, or whatever they call it. He constantly calls me *sir*, or *Master Luke*. Don't get me wrong, it's not that I'm into titles. It's just that I kind of like being treated with respect for a change.

As for Artoo — well, I know I should be annoyed with him for lying to me and running off. But he did it for a good reason, and if he hadn't,

I'd most likely be dead now, and he and Three-pio would be spare parts. He seems like a cheerful sort of fellow, and imaginative, too.

If anything happened to the two of them, I'd miss them. Since they were both hijacked by Jawas, I don't think I have any real title to them, but they feel like family droids, and thus my responsibility. I warned them to keep their eyes open and stay alert, and then I followed Ben into the cantina.

I was lost in the place. I stared around, realizing that there was a lot going on. People and aliens were sitting around talking, exchanging information and packages and other things. A lot of it had to be illegal, but it was being done right out in the open.

I must have looked like an easy target to some of the regulars there. I mean, staring around with an amazed expression on my face and all. A couple of heavy types came over to me. The human was nasty. I'm not even sure what his companion was; I've never seen an alien like him before. Anyway, they started to pick a fight with me for absolutely no reason.

I didn't know what to do, and I guess that showed, too. They started to push and yell at me — and I just stood there and took it. What else could I do? I didn't want to start a fight, and they weren't listening to anything I had to say.

One of them shoved me to the floor and went for a blaster. And I could see that he intended to use it!

I don't know what his problem was, but I suspect he was simply bored and wanted to kill somebody for fun.

It was scary, but I didn't really have time to think about it. Ben came out of nowhere, and tried to calm the creeps down. It didn't work, and the human went for his blaster again.

I've never in my life seen anything as fast as what happened next. Ben somehow had his own lightsaber out, and it was *slicing* before anyone had a chance to breathe. One swipe, and the man's arm was cut off! His alien friend had time for a squeal before his chest was sliced, too.

I was just astounded at how fast Ben had moved. I'd barely blinked, and it was all over. He simply shrugged and promised me that one day I'd do the same, while also making it very clear that violence is to be used as a last resort. I can see why he'd be a great teacher.

Anyway, he'd found us a contact — a Wookiee named Chewbacca. You'd think I wouldn't be shocked by anything at this point. But Chewie sure managed to surprise me. He's one of the tallest beings I've ever seen in my life, and definitely the hairiest. Wookiees are all hair and fangs — and *muscles*. He was one tough-looking alien. Amazingly, Ben could actually speak a little of his language, so we could talk.

My first thought, looking at him, was that Chewie had to be some important guy's bodyguard. He didn't wear clothing — with all of that hair, he certainly didn't need any! — but he had a bandolier slung over his shoulder, a blaster at his hip, and a bowcaster on his back. He was a walking showcase of muscle and weaponry. Talk about reeking of hired gun, I thought.

I was wrong.

It turned out that Chewie is the first mate of a Corellian stock light freighter named the *Millennium Falcon.* He was obviously a lot brighter than he looked, which taught me not to make snap judgments. He suggested that we wait while he found his captain, so Ben and I did just that. Aside from anything else, I wouldn't want to argue with a Wookiee.

He was back pretty soon with a Corellian. They're humans, and this one wasn't that much bigger than I am, but . . . well, there's something about him. He's kind of cocky and self-assured, and more than a little flippant. But you can see, immediately, that he's kind of special.

It's in the way he holds himself, I guess. Like he knows the galaxy's against him, and he doesn't care. He'll take whatever is thrown at him and come out swinging. He had a blaster, hung low on his hip, kind of gunfighter style, and a casual manner about his dress, his speech, and his way of doing things. This was Han Solo, captain of the *Millennium Falcon.*

Ben seemed to like him right away, and they started negotiating.

Early on I gathered a few things about Captain Solo. First, he and Chewie are the only crew of the ship. Second, Solo is a smuggler. I don't have much of a problem with that; I guess some goods are essential to almost all known worlds, and the Empire imposes some pretty outrageous taxes. Most people don't consider smugglers to be serious criminals, but they're generally reckoned to be pretty dangerous customers. They're avoided for the most part. It's a profession that attracts people with big egos, who take big chances and who reap big profits . . .

Or death.

The Imperials don't like their taxes being avoided, and they hunt out spice smugglers. Nobody in a place like this cantina would ever turn in a spice runner, but with all the stormtroopers in the city, one whiff of any contraband spice and Solo could be fried in a second. Still, you don't get to be very old in the spice trade if you're not fast on your feet and faster with your wits. Solo looked old enough to be both of these.

Luckily, Solo didn't much care that the Imperials were after us; it sort of put us on equal footing — as renegades. The problem was, he wanted a spice profit for a flight to Alderaan. Ten thousand credits!

That was *way* out of our league, and Ben knew it. But it didn't seem to bother him. He made a counteroffer of two thousand upfront, and another fifteen at Alderaan. He was obviously planning to get it from the princess, which made sense. I mean, she's a princess, right? She's bound to have more money than even she can spend. Of course, we still had to come up with two thousand. I had about thirty in my pockets, and Ben didn't have a single coin. He said he always managed to get along without any. I can't see how, myself, but I'm starting to learn that Ben's pretty different from most people.

We left Solo and Chewie at the cantina and headed over to a used speeder lot with Artoo and Threepio. As usual, the dealer tried to cut us down in price, and Ben's use of the Force saved us again. We needed two thousand for Captain Solo, and that's what Ben got us. I'm sure the dealer's going to wonder why he was so generous when he recovers, but he can still sell the landspeeder at a profit, so we didn't feel too badly.

Then we headed for the docking bay where Solo has his ship. In the cantina, he told us how fast it was, and how trim, and how . . . well, pretty much what a wonder it was. I should have known better than to believe everything he said, of course. When I saw the *Falcon*, I could tell it was a piece of junk.

It was worn down, rebuilt, and jury-rigged. You could see the weld marks, the mismatched pieces, the forced-together technology. It looked like one serious landing would shake the ship to pieces. But Ben only smiled, like this was exactly what he'd expected. I can't figure him out sometimes. I was sure we were being conned.

Then Solo and the Wookiee appeared, and we headed for the ship for takeoff. That's when the stormtroopers took us by surprise.

Maybe the ones Ben had fooled had come to their senses. Maybe they had sniffed the spices. Maybe they were just plain lucky and were checking out the spaceport on the off chance of finding their droids skipping the planet. Whatever the reason, they saw us and started firing.

I have to hand it to Solo and Chewie — they certainly know what to do when blasters are firing. They had us all aboard, the door locked, and the *Falcon* powered before the Imperials even managed to get close to us. Ben and I strapped in, Artoo and Threepio plugged in, and Solo and Chewie took us up faster than even I imagined possible.

But that didn't get us out of trouble. There were Imperial cruisers in orbit — waiting for us.

This was the first time I'd ever been off Tatooine, but I didn't get the chance to enjoy it because the *Falcon* was dodging shots. Everything was exploding all around us, and we were getting thrown around like crazy. Artificial gravity has its drawbacks, and one is that it takes a few microseconds to switch back and forth when the ship's on violent maneuvers. Solo must have been at least half the pilot he claimed to be, because he dodged the fighters and took us to lightspeed.

And I was too shaken up to really appreciate it. But the change was still absolutely incredible. The universe goes all weird and then — *wham!* Lightspeed, and everything's still, like you're not moving.

Time in lightspeed isn't really like time in the rest of the universe. There, time ticks away on chronos and things happen. Once you break the light barrier, though, it's not that simple. I don't understand the physics very well — I'm not sure anyone does, really — but you can work out exactly how far and how long you need to go in which direction to get you to where you're going.

I just hoped that Solo or Chewie could plot a course the way they could dodge Imperial cruisers. If they could, everything would be fine.

All my life, I've longed for something to happen to me. Something important. And now that it has, I'm not sure how to handle it. I'm glad to be off Tatooine. But I still haven't seen anything of the stars, or the galaxy at large. And, to be honest, I'm really just a passenger along for the ride. Ben says he needs my help, but I haven't been much help so far. He had to save me in the cantina, and it's Solo and Chewie who got us off Tatooine.

Maybe I'll have something to do soon, other than practice trying to use the Force. Not that this isn't a great challenge. Ben has already taught me the basics, like the proper grip and ready position. I never realized how important body positioning is. The idea is to start with just the right stance, so you're immediately ready for attack or defense. And to avoid standing with your feet too wide apart, which kills your speed and agility. As Ben says, you must feel your center of balance.

My training consists of lots of drills. Mostly using my lightsaber against a seeker robot.

The robot sends out laser bolts and I have to ward them off — which is no easy feat. And when I'm done with the drills, I'm instructed to visualize them!

Sometimes Ben stands behind me and guides me as I move from the first to the fourth defensive postures. As I listen to Ben's voice, I try to empty my thoughts of everything, to use wide circular motions, fluid and confident, and to parry with a *full* movement. By focusing on the pattern of the drill, I'm supposed to tune the world out. That's the goal: to let go of all rational thought and allow the Force to do the work.

Unfortunately, it feels like *I'm* doing all the work. So, to help me get the hang of it, Ben had me use my lightsaber — while blindfolded! I had to just let go and feel. And guess what? I really sensed something. Some sort of energy. It was incredible! It was almost as though I could see in my mind's eye which way to move. Maybe Ben's right and I do have some aptitude for the Force — like my father had.

I hope so. I don't want to be in some great quest and great adventure and end up just being a passenger. I want to be able to do my share.

EIGHTH ENTRY

Just when I thought things couldn't get any worse, they've really plummeted.

Ben's dead.

I'm still trying to sort out my thoughts and feelings. I mean, I'd only known Ben for a day, really. Yet I miss him even more than I miss my aunt and uncle . . . and I spent my life with them.

There was just something so special, so alive about Ben. Being around him was like being around the father I had never had . . . but always dreamed about.

And now he's gone.

Ben was teaching me so much about the Force, and without him, I don't know if I'll ever hear about it again. So I'd better record what I can remember, while it's still fresh in my mind.

If Ben was the last Jedi, then I'll never become one. But I know what I have learned from Ben has made a huge difference in my life. I can feel the power around me and within me. I know his teachings are important enough to hold on to. And pass along.

Ben and I spoke a lot about the Force — the energy force created by all living things. Ben called it "an aura that at once controls and obeys," although he said no one, not even the Jedi Masters or scientists, could find a true definition for it. I guess that's because it's *in* one's mind as much as outside of it. It's not something you can put your finger on to control and study. You have to believe in its power to access its power.

Anyway, if this seems confusing, that's okay. Nobody understands it right away. Ben said that learning the Force requires great patience — that it's a lifelong education. He seemed to think that even at his age and level of mastery, he was still learning.

Once, Ben said, the Jedi-in-training would spend a great deal of time contemplating and opening themselves gradually to the Force. But that's when the Jedi were the leaders of the galaxy and the keepers of the peace. Things have changed. There's no time for that now. Ben wanted me to train in a faster way. A more active, hands-on approach. Still, the essential teachings are as they always were. Learn to trust the Force. Learn to open up the senses and *feel* the Force.

Sometimes I think I can do this. But other times I'm not so sure. Ben told me to trust my feelings and to let go of trying to control myself. There are times when I have to divorce my actions from conscious control. I'm not exactly sure when to do this, but Ben said I'll know when the time comes.

The workings of the Force aren't always direct, but they're strong. Because of it, Ben knew I was coming and would need his help when the Sand People struck. Somehow, if you're open, the Force gives you information. Like knowing when someone is following you without actually seeing anyone. It's a lot like having a sixth sense, really.

It can also help you influence the weak-minded, or those accustomed to obeying orders, like the stormtroopers. Ben demonstrated this numerous times. He would say something with such total confidence that others would believe anything he said — even *repeat* what he had said. It was unbelievable! It was like Ben hypnotized them.

I think one of the hardest lessons for me is not to be fooled by appearances. Ben looked like a shabby old hermit, but that wasn't the truth. The *Falcon* looks like a pile of junk, but that's not the truth, either. I have to confess, if my friends were around, I would have felt ashamed of Ben and the *Falcon* upon first glance. But I'm learning that appearances don't count for much. Imperial troops look smart and impressive, but at heart they're just cowards and bullies.

Ben told me that the Force can accomplish miracles. That anything is possible when you are open to the Force and you let it flow through you. That's how I'm supposed to use my lightsaber — let it *flow* from me. It's all about letting yourself go and trusting the Force.

Of course, very few men recognize or feel

the Force. And even fewer can use it. But a Jedi feels the Force, just like any other physical object. A Jedi can harness its power.

One of the most important things Ben taught me is that if one man suffers, all men suffer. If evil is not stopped, it will rule over *all* men one day — whether they've opposed it or ignored it. And so, with Ben's teachings under my belt, I mark my next challenge: to fight for justice against evil and tyranny.

I've always been afraid that I'd be stuck on a farm my whole life. But that's no longer the case. For one thing, the farm's gone. For another, I can feel a difference inside me. Maybe it's the Force. Maybe it's just everything I've been through. But I'm not the same Luke Skywalker I was just a few days ago.

It's so bizarre. Not much has happened in my life that's worth remembering. And yet, in just two days, everything's completely changed. I found a living link to my father, and lost him. And I even managed to rescue a princess on the way.

I'd better do this the way I've been doing everything, and that's to try to tell it in order, and make some sense out of what happened. So here goes . . .

On the way to Alderaan, I kept busy with my exercises — especially deflecting the laserbolts from the seeker. I was excited to learn and was moving at an exhausting rate. But I couldn't stop thinking about my aunt and uncle. What happened to them was so sick. So painful. At the time I didn't realize how much my anger was building. Or that I should watch out for something like that. Most people would have told me I deserved to be upset, and that it was perfectly normal to feel this way.

But Ben warned me how easy and natural it could be to turn to anger, fear, and aggression — the dark side of the Force. He could see the anger in me, and the revenge I wanted on the Empire and Darth Vader for what they'd done to my family. Ben told me that such emotions are very strong, but that they tap into the dark side of the Force. And by entering the dark side, you strengthen its hold on the evil in yourself. "If you give in to those feelings," he promised me, "then you give in to the dark side. You will become like Darth Vader."

That's the scary thought; I wouldn't want to end up like that. But, at the same time, I don't know how I'll ever be able to give up my anger and desire for revenge. Vader and the others *must* pay for what they've done. I don't know if Ben really understood what he was asking of me. He said that he did, that he had to give up his own quest for vengeance, too. I guess he meant when Vader killed my father. I know that upset Ben a lot.

So what do I do? I don't want to end up seduced by the dark side. But I want to see Vader pay for his crimes. If the Force is with me, Ben said the correct path will become clear. I really hope so, because I could use a little clarity right now.

As I was thinking about this, Ben gave a cry and almost collapsed.

He assured me he was all right, but that he'd felt a great disturbance in the Force. Like a billion voices all crying out at once. He said he'd never felt anything like it before, and I could see that it bothered him. He didn't know what had caused it.

I was afraid that the strain of everything was getting to be too much for him. I didn't know how old Ben was, but he certainly wasn't used to all of this activity anymore.

I should have known better by then — that Ben was stronger than he looked — but I didn't completely trust Ben's feeling for the Force.

Then Han said we were ready to come out of lightspeed near Alderaan. That was really exciting news, because I was picturing us landing at the royal palace, being greeted as honored guests . . . maybe even dining with royalty, that sort of thing.

But the *Millennium Falcon* didn't come out into normal space next to Alderaan as planned. We came out of lightspeed in an asteroid belt, rocks of all shapes and sizes whizzing all around us. Han had to do some tricky flying to avoid getting us smashed to bits.

My first thought, of course, was that he'd messed up his navigation. But the truth was a lot worse than that. I could see that we were close to Alderaan's star, and this was where Alderaan should have been. . . .

But it wasn't.

It took us a while to realize what we were seeing, and longer to accept the truth: the rubble and rocks were all that was left of Alderaan.

That was the disturbance in the Force that Ben had felt, the voices all crying out at once: the cry of all the people on Alderaan just before they died.

Now we were in serious trouble. I mean, we were stunned by the planet's destruction and the deaths of all those people. It didn't seem real somehow. I'd never been to Alderaan, but I've heard it was lovely and peaceful. And now it was dust and rocks, everyone on the planet gone.

What were we going to do now? The message from Princess Leia had told us to take the droids to her father, and that he'd know what to do with them. Now her father was dead. Han still needed to be paid, and we couldn't cover the charge. All of these thoughts were whirling about in my head as we came under the attack of a TIE fighter.

This was the first time I'd ever seen a TIE in action. It's sort of dumpy, with stubby wings, but it sure can move. This one fired off a single burst at us, and then ran for it. Han started to chase him, then realized something important. TIE fighters can't go to lightspeed, so they always have Imperial cruisers nearby. But there weren't any around. So where was this one from?

The answer was literally right in front of us. We all thought it was a small moon at first. As we got closer, though, we realized it wasn't a small anything — it was a huge round space station.

And it had an unbreakable tractor beam that grabbed hold of the *Falcon* and dragged her in.

We were in serious, serious trouble. The question in our minds was whether this had destroyed Alderaan. And it now had a hold of us. Did they know we were heading here? Had they destroyed the planet to stop us from reaching it? Or had we just accidentally stumbled onto something that had nothing to do with us?

Ben and Han came up with a plan. Because of Han's smuggling, the *Falcon* is equipped with hidden compartments to hide illegal cargo in case he's boarded and searched. Instead of cargo, though, he planned to hide all of us. He rigged the records to make it look like we'd all abandoned ship at Tatooine and left the *Falcon* to make the jump to hyperspace herself. With any luck, the troopers would believe this story and go back to hunting for us on Tatooine.

Well, the first part of our plan worked without a hitch. We hid while the Imperials pulled the *Falcon* into the docking bay. Troopers came aboard and searched. They found the doctored log, and no sign of any of us in the sealed and lined compartments. They fell for the story and all filed out.

I was glad to get out of the hiding place. Being in a confined space with a Wookiee can result in serious bruising. They don't like being cramped. We were free for now, but it wouldn't last. We needed an escape plan, and Ben came up with one.

There had to be a tractor beam holding us in place. He'd deactivate it, and then the *Falcon* could take off. That is, if we weren't chased by TIE fighters or whatever else this huge station had on board. It wasn't much of a plan, but it was all we had, so even Han agreed to it.

He wasn't happy about it, though.

The troopers had left, but they were bound to be back. So when two of them returned, Han and Chewie took them by surprise — and stunned them both. I winced at the noise they made, but nobody else seemed to notice.

Ben had Han and me dress up in the trooper's armor and stand guard. That way, it looked like we were real guards on duty. The only problem was that I'm under the height requirements for an Imperial trooper. The uniform was kind of loose on me. Still, if I was seen at a distance I looked passable. I hoped!

We all snuck into a small command office near the *Falcon.* The gantry officer inside was taken out by a blow from Chewie and a blast from Han. With all the noise they were making, I thought we'd be found for sure.

Artoo managed to plug into the station's computer. Like I've said before, he's really smart and great at mechanical stuff. He broke into the station files and discovered where the main controls for the tractor beam were, so Ben could go off and sabotage them.

Before he left, Ben said something about detecting a familiar pattern in the Force. I didn't pay much attention to it then, but later I realized what had happened: Ben had detected Darth Vader on board! He didn't tell me because he was afraid I'd go running off to try to kill him. If I'd known, that's exactly what I'd have done. It's a good thing Ben didn't tell me, because I might be dead right now.

Instead, Ben told us to stay put. I had intended to obey him, but things changed. I mean, I wanted revenge on the Empire for what they'd done to my uncle and aunt, those innocent Jawas, and the whole planet of Alderaan. But I wasn't stupid. This space station was the size of a small moon — not small at all. There had to be thousands of people on board. So trying to take them on for revenge was definitely the last thought on my mind.

But then See-Threepio translated Artoo's excited beeping. He kept saying, "I've found her!" and "She's here!" I've never seen a droid look so excited in my life, and it took a couple of minutes to get him calmed down to the point where he could tell us what he meant.

It was Princess Leia Organa he was talking about. Somehow, she was aboard the station, in the detention area! I couldn't believe it. I mean, she'd been on that ship that had been attacked over Tatooine. I wasn't sure whether she'd escaped or been captured or what, but I had never expected her to be here, of all places. On the station that had probably destroyed her home planet and all of her family, too.

And she was going to be next. Artoo told us that there was a termination order on her. They planned to execute her!

That was when I made up my mind that it was time for me to act. So far, all I'd really done was hang around and follow orders — mostly Ben's, but with some of Han's thrown in, too. But I *couldn't* let them kill the princess. Mostly, I think, because she was just too beautiful to let that sort of thing happen to her. Also because she had been relying on Ben to help her out. Ben knew her and obviously admired her. I had to do something to get her free.

There was no way I could do that on my own. But if Han were to help me, I thought maybe we could manage it. Han complains a lot, but he's really good with a blaster, and can be very inventive . . . especially when he's in a tight spot.

So all I had to do was to convince him to help me rescue the princess. Well, the word *princess* alone grabbed his interest. He refused to risk his neck, though, until I pointed out that she was rich and would obviously give him a big reward for his help. I didn't mention that probably most of her wealth had gone up in smoke with Alderaan. The thought of more money helped swing him around — and he agreed to help me rescue her!

It was up to me to come up with a plan. Before this, most of my plans were simple things like how to fix broken farm machinery, or how to pull a joke on Windy back home. Now I had to outthink Imperial troopers and rescue the princess from her jail cell, which was bound to be guarded.

But then I realized something: *we* were guards.

And instantly I knew how we could get into the detention area. I explained my plan to Han and Chewie. The Wookiee complained loudly, because it involved his looking like he was our prisoner. If we were taking him into the cells for some crime, the other guards would let us in. Then we would be able to get to the princess's cell and get her out.

Of course, *then* we'd have to get back to the *Falcon* with her, hoping that nobody noticed. I thought that on a ship this size, there had to be women workers, so maybe a princess wouldn't stick out like a sore thumb. Of course, that was before I knew the Empire *rarely* uses women or aliens in their forces. That's how narrow-minded Vader and the rest are. They don't think women are useful!

Anyway, instead I decided to concentrate on one problem at a time. When we had the princess safe, the rest of the plan could be worked out.

With any luck, that was.

Despite Chewie's complaints, Han managed to convince him that my idea was good. We took him to an elevator bank wearing unlocked restraints. And nobody seemed to think we were anything other than two guards with a prisoner. Some of them gave the Wookiee odd looks, but nobody asked us questions or stopped us.

Until we reached the detention area, of course. There we ran into a major problem. There was an officer on duty at the entrance, and he was your typical Imperial by-the-book type. He wanted transfer papers and all sorts of authorizations for Chewie that we obviously didn't have. There were a couple of guards with him, and they were starting to get suspicious.

Luckily, Han thinks fast. He had Chewie stage a breakout, and while everyone was staring at the mad Wookiee, he and I managed to shoot the guards. Unfortunately, not before the officer sounded the alarm.

I found out where the princess was being held and headed straight for her cell. Han and Chewie stayed behind to try and sort out the mess we'd caused. I was feeling the adrenaline pumping now, after that fight. I didn't know whether I'd killed the guards I'd shot or simply stunned them. To be honest, I didn't really care.

I'd have thought I'd have felt worse about killing someone, but right then I had more important things on my mind. Besides, the guard would have killed me, so it was definitely self-defense. And yes, he was holding and would have killed the princess. But he was also a human being, somebody with a family who maybe loved him. And maybe I'd killed him. It's a really odd feeling, thinking about that.

But right then I was occupied with other things. Such as saving a princess.

I found her cell door and opened it without any problem. She was awake inside, and obviously expecting to be taken off for execution. She looked up at me, and all the things I'd been planning to say went right out of my head.

She was even more beautiful in person than she'd looked on the recording. There was a look in her eyes that told me she'd never beg for her life, and that she'd fight to the end to stay alive. So all of my *Hi, I'm Luke Skywalker, and this is a rescue* lines went clean out of my head. I just stood there, stammering a little.

And she asked me, "Aren't you a little short for a stormtrooper?" Like that was the only thing on her mind right then.

It was such an odd thing to say that it started my brain working again. I managed to tell her who I was, and I took off the helmet. That was so she could see my face and tell I was being truthful. It was also so I could get a better look at her. The eyepieces in the helmet were a little distorting.

She didn't know who I was, of course, so I explained that we had her Artoo unit, and that we were there with Ben Kenobi. *That* got her attention, and she started to ask questions I didn't have time to answer.

Suddenly there was a whole bunch of firing, and Han and Chewie came down the tunnel toward us, firing their guns behind them. It seemed that Han hadn't managed to convince security that there wasn't a problem, and there were more guards pouring into the area, all after us.

The princess wasn't exactly thrilled with this news, and Han was even less thrilled with the princess. I could see that they'd both taken an instant dislike to one another. But they didn't have too much time to express their differences. We were trapped inside a maximum security area, with guards coming at us from the only exit.

It was not a good place to be right then.

had to cut that last entry short to relieve Han for a while at the controls of the *Millennium Falcon.* And, to be honest, because I'm getting to the part I really dread — Ben's death. But I've simply got to steel myself and get on with it. This way, I can try to get a handle on how I feel.

Well, Leia — she asked me to stop calling her *princess* because she hates formality — realized that I'd messed things up. "You call this a rescue?" she demanded.

I suppose I should have been annoyed that she wasn't more grateful; Han certainly was irritated. After all, she'd been marked for execution, and we were doing our best to get her out alive. The problem was, there didn't seem to be any way to escape all those stormtroopers. Han looked to me for a plan; I didn't have anyone to look to.

And I was fresh out of ideas.

Leia wasn't, though. I'd always pictured princesses as these pampered young women with great skin, gorgeous bodies, rich fathers, and brains permanently in neutral. But Leia's nothing like that. Well, no, that's not what I mean. She *is* beautiful, but she's not pampered or spoiled, and her brain is obviously *very* active.

She grabbed my blaster and blew a hole in the tunnel wall. I didn't know why, until she explained that it was the way the garbage went out, and if garbage went out, so could we. It sounded pretty reasonable, but with blaster bolts burning up the air from the troopers, almost anything would have sounded pretty reasonable right then. We didn't have much choice but to follow her in.

There was a drop, and then thick, garbage-strewn water. What there wasn't was a door out of there. The smell was awful, and I didn't even want to think about what might be floating around with us. The water was about waist-deep; at least, I *hoped* it was water.

Then things got really bad.

There was something alive in there. I don't know what, because we never actually saw it. There were only low-level lights in the place, so we saw mostly shapes and shadows. But whatever it was, it was big and it was aquatic. And, apparently, it ate almost anything. The Imperials must use it to get rid of organic wastes, which made sense. Anyway, the problem with that was that *we* were organic, and the thing went for us.

Specifically, for me.

Tentacles suddenly wrapped around me, and I was dragged under the water. I had just enough warning to allow me to gulp in a lungful of air. But I lost my blaster as I was yanked off my feet. I did have my lightsaber, but it was inside the armor I wore, and I didn't think the monster that had me would allow me to get it out. I struggled in the dark, filthy water, trying to free myself, and trying not to breathe.

I'll admit that I was scared stiff. There's nothing worse than fighting something you can't see, in slow motion because you're underwater. I wanted to scream, and couldn't. It was just me and this thing in the darkness.

Then I felt . . . its *tongue*, I guess. Something that rubbed along my armor and then across my face. I wanted to vomit, but I was too busy holding my breath. It felt rough, like sand grains on the skin.

And then it just let me go.

I don't know why. Thinking back, the most obvious reason is that it's a scavenger. It eats refuse. And I was alive, kicking — quite a lot —

and a lot warmer than its normal food. I just didn't suit its taste, so it let me go.

I staggered to my feet and took in a deep breath. I almost wished I hadn't, because then I could tell what I smelled like, and it was *awful.* But I was so glad to be alive, I didn't really care.

Then suddenly, we heard the sound of motors. I'd heard something rumbling while I was underwater, and probably the whatever-it-was under there had, too. Maybe that's why it let me go: it knew what those noises meant, and it had some way out of the room.

We didn't get it at first.

We weren't just in a garbage chute; we'd fallen into a trash compactor. And we were going to get compacted along with the garbage!

I don't know if the Imperials did this deliberately, or whether the compactor was simply running on a regular schedule. Either way, our luck had run bad. The walls were closing in, and we were destined to become a lot thinner.

We all panicked and tried to jam the walls apart. We didn't have any luck, naturally. Things were starting to look really bad for us again, and Han and Leia were trading insults as the walls got closer.

Then the comlink sounded, and Threepio was on the other end. He and Artoo had run into some trouble, but I didn't have time for any long-winded stories. I ordered him to have Artoo shut down the trash compactors and then open the door for us — fast!

It was an incredible relief to get out of there. We smelled repulsive, of course, and the body gloves Han and I still wore under the white stormtrooper armor were wet.

Somehow — even after falling into the trash — Leia managed to look lovely. Apparently, Han was too busy arguing with her to notice.

I was hoping we'd have an easy, uneventful trip back to the *Falcon.* But the stormtroopers had other ideas. They were after us again. We had no choice but to run for it and try to get to the ship from another direction. Somehow Leia and I got separated from Han and Chewie in the fighting and running. But at least we were armed with guns — which made us feel a bit better.

The troopers' armor is supposed to reflect blaster bolts. That's why they wear it in the first place. Only there are several weak spots you can hit if you're a good-enough shot. The joints, for example, or the neck. And if you aim just right, the eyepieces. Most of the Imperials weren't very good shots. Maybe because they're used to just rounding people up and murdering them, which doesn't take much skill. They had a hard time shooting at us, because we ducked and weaved and shot back a lot. I was a pretty decent shot back home — when you've got little else to do, you tend to practice shooting a lot. So most of the troopers I hit stayed down. What surprised me was that Leia was good, too. She'd obviously practiced a lot as well.

Our luck couldn't hold, of course. Sooner or later we'd run into someone who actually could shoot straight. Leia and I ducked through a door and shot out the lock behind us, only to discover we'd sealed ourselves *into* trouble, not out of it.

We were at the top of a drop shaft, leading into the depths of the station. I don't know how far down it went, but it had to be *kilometers*. This was a big station. There was a door on the other side of the drop, and absolutely no way to get over to it. There was a ramp that could be extended across the drop — providing we hadn't already shot out the controls, of course.

So we were stuck, and the troopers knew it. All they had to do was blast through the door and push us off.

I wasn't about to panic, though, and make the princess think I was a jerk. Instead, I considered our options. There was nothing to make a bridge out of, but my eye caught a length of piping about ten feet above where we stood.

We *might* be able to swing across.

In my belt I had several items that were

handy around the farm, one of which was a spool of cable. It's very high-tensile, because you never knew when you might need to pull a stuck droid out of a moisture sump or something. And there was a small hook on the end, enabling it to snap into place and hold on. So I took it out and flung it over the bar above us. It clicked and caught hold.

"Hang on!" I told Leia.

She understood what I was doing and grabbed me tightly. I wished I had longer to appreciate that hold, then she abruptly kissed me.

"For luck!" she explained.

Well, we certainly needed all the luck we could get. The touch of her lips burned on my cheek, and I took a deep breath and swung.

We made it, even if my landing was a bit wobbly. Then Leia opened the door and we were heading back to the ship. The Imperials still didn't have the far door open, so they didn't know we'd made it to the other side.

I was still all mixed-up inside as I ran with the princess. She'd *kissed* me! Okay, it was only a peck on the cheek, but she was the only woman who'd ever kissed me. Oh, Aunt Beru had when I was a child, but relatives don't count. It made me feel so good. The princess was starting to like me! And I was crazy about her, of course.

I'd never known anyone quite like her. Leia has such a directness about her, such a certainty that what she's doing is right. She doesn't see her rank as one giving her rights, but as one giving her opportunities. You can't help admiring her.

Well, I can't, anyway.

Han can't understand why she's fighting for the Rebels. She's rich! He says that what's important in life is money, and that's all he wants. Maybe that's what he believes himself, but I don't. I think there's more to Han Solo than he wants people to see. Oh, he's certainly interested in money, but I don't think he's as selfish as he pretends to be. He couldn't be that shallow.

I may as well admit that I'm talking so much here because I don't really want to talk about what happened next. But I can't keep avoiding it, no matter how painful it is. So I'll just take a deep breath and move on. . . .

We made it back to the docking bay at about the same time as Han and Chewie. The droids were there, too, but Ben wasn't back yet. Han and Chewie ran to the *Falcon.* Leia, of course, stared at it the way I had when I'd first seen it.

"You came here in that?" she asked us. "You're braver than I thought."

I'd figured it out by now, and tried to explain to her that Han *deliberately* made the ship look like it was junk. That way, when the *Falcon* zipped right past the Imperials, they'd be caught completely by surprise. I didn't get far with my explanation because I suddenly felt this chill clean down to my bones. I turned around. Shocked, I saw Ben with his lightsaber activated.

His opponent was a figure I'll never forget. He wore black armor and a long, black cloak. He was taller by a head than Ben, and obviously tremendously strong. Yet Ben was holding him off without too much effort.

Ben must have run into trouble while he was fixing the tractor beam. He caught sight of us as he fought and gave a nod to show he'd fixed it. We could leave.

Except we couldn't abandon Ben, of course.

The person he was fighting could only be one man. I realized now that Ben had felt him when we'd landed. It had to be Darth Vader, the man who'd killed my father. I stared at him with hatred and loathing — not caring what Ben had said about such emotions laying you open to the dark side of the Force.

With everything I had inside me, I willed Ben to kill him.

And Ben knew this. I could tell. He could feel me through the Force. Then he did the most unbelievable, most *idiotic* thing he could have done.

He broke apart from Vader and said a few words to him. Then he raised his lightsaber — not to fight, but as a kind of mocking salute.

I couldn't believe it! Ben had been winning, and he simply gave up!

Vader took advantage of Ben's move, of course. He didn't do anything noble or quixotic like saluting back. He brought his own lightsaber down over his head and right through Ben.

At least, that's what *should* have happened. There should have been two pieces of Ben, sliced nearly down the middle, lying on the deck.

Instead, there was just the rustle of his cloak settling to the deck.

I didn't understand it then, and I don't understand it now. Somehow, Ben's body had simply *vanished.* Vader had won the fight, but he didn't have anything to show for it except Ben's cloak and his deactivated lightsaber, rolling across the deck.

It didn't matter. Ben was *dead.* I simply went crazy. Right then and there, all I wanted to do was to attack Vader and kill him. I just wanted to rush over there and take Vader apart, piece by piece. Despite the troopers that had appeared and were shooting at us. They somehow seemed unimportant to me. It never occurred to me that they might actually be able to kill me.

Only two things stopped me from getting myself killed. First of all, the *Falcon* was ready to lift off, and Han and Leia were ready to go with it. They weren't going to let me stay behind and die. I fought to get free of them, to go and avenge Ben, but I was still sane enough not to want to hurt them.

And then it happened.

I heard Ben's voice, quietly, in my ear, as definitely as I've ever heard anyone's voice in my life.

"Run, Luke, run!" he ordered.

I didn't even think about it then. If Ben wanted me to go, I'd do it. I turned and dashed into the ship. Han had her up and heading for the doors before I could even sit down. Luckily, the doors were on a proximity alert and opened as the *Falcon* approached them. Ben had indeed fixed the tractor beam, and we were off and away.

We had a new passenger now — Princess Leia Organa. But we'd left one behind in payment.

Why?

Why, when he could have won, did he let Vader kill him? I couldn't understand it. It made absolutely no sense to me at all. If he'd done it to stop Vader from reaching us, maybe I could have accepted that. Ben giving his life to let us get away — yes, that would have been heroic. But that wasn't it at all. He could have killed Vader, I'm sure of it. But he *didn't*. Why?

Ben had to have almost as much reason to hate Vader as I did. Vader killed my father, his best friend. Vader betrayed the Jedi and led them to their deaths. Vader works for the Emperor, an evil man who victimizes the weak and helpless. And Vader, I learned from Leia, was the one in charge of the Tatooine troopers who killed my uncle and aunt.

It all comes back to Vader.

So why didn't Ben kill him?

Leia says that the Jedi work in mysterious ways. But I don't understand. It's bad enough that Ben's dead, but I don't know *why* he's dead, and that makes it worse.

Only . . . *is* he dead, exactly? I'm certain I heard his voice there in the hangar. I know he spoke to me after he'd been killed. And that doesn't make sense, either.

Oh, I've heard stories and legends about spirits, people coming back after they're dead. But Ben certainly hadn't seen the spirits of the billions of people who died on Alderaan. He *felt* their deaths as a great disturbance in the Force.

I felt nothing when Ben died. Nothing physical, that is. It stabbed me to the heart. But if I'm as strong in the Force as Ben claims, shouldn't I have felt it when he died?

Ben, *why* did you do it?

How can I go forward without you?

Things are moving *so* fast!

I don't have time to think everything through, but my life has changed so drastically over the past few days that I'm definitely not the same person I was. I'm having to adapt so quickly, to change my beliefs and aims and to continually fight just to stay alive.

One thing of which there's no doubt: I'm a part of the Rebellion now. I guess I knew I was when I saw my aunt and uncle dead on Tatooine. I had to fight against anyone who could do that kind of thing. But now I'm an *official* Rebel, because we've caught up with the Rebel Alliance, here on the fourth moon of Yavin.

It's hard to picture a world less like Tatooine. There, everywhere you look is desert, with maybe a small town here or there. It's a continuous fight to suck the water we need from the almost-dry air. This moon, however, is a forest, vast and luxurious. Instead of bleak browns and scorched whites, the planet is a riot of green and life. I've heard of such worlds before, but to actually stand on one of them. . . .

This is my first alien planet! Okay, technically, it's a moon of the big gas giant Yavin. But it's so much more wonderful than Tatooine. Not many people live here right now. There are all these vast ruins of some ancient civilization, and the Rebellion has taken one over to use as its base. The only problem is, the Empire now knows we're here.

I'd better pick up where I left off before, to explain this.

We got away from the Death Star — that's what the Imperials call that gigantic space station of theirs — only to be attacked by TIE fighters. Naturally, though, the *Millennium Falcon* is equipped with guns. Han took the top turret, and I took the lower one, while Chewie piloted us.

And then came one of the most intense few minutes of my life.

It's one thing to do target practice, or to zap womp rats from a T-16, but it's *very* different shooting at something that can shoot back at you. The TIE fighters came in fast and nasty. Han and I just kept firing while Chewie dodged as best he could. I didn't do too well at first, but then I got the hang of it. Han and I eventually got them all, and the *Falcon* escaped into light-speed!

That's when we finally learned what was going on. Leia was behind a lot of the events, it turned out. She's an Imperial Senator, and knows enough to be appalled at what the Emperor was doing. She told Han and me a whole string of terrible things — from random arrests and beatings all the way to the destruction of Alderaan.

Leia decided to join the Rebellion, and soon became one of its top leaders. She's very strong, and she's obviously bottling up her own grief now because there's a job to be done.

I'm trying to do the same myself. There's no time to cry over the dead when there are so many more living who might join them if we don't do our jobs.

Anyway, then Leia learned about the Death Star. One Rebel agent managed to get the complete plans for it, which Leia was delivering to the Rebel base when Darth Vader and his men intercepted her. She fed the plans into Artoo, along with the message to Ben. Then the droids escaped, but she was captured. She didn't say what happened next, except that Grand Moff Tarkin, who's in charge of the Death Star, blew up Alderaan as a warning. Now he's after this Rebel base, hoping to finish off the Rebellion. And he can do it, too. Leia

says that the Death Star is almost unstop-
pable.

And it's that *almost* we have to count on.

Leia realized that Vader had let the *Falcon*
go, hiding a homing beacon onboard her. So
they must know where we are. That's why we
were able to make our getaway "so easily." It
didn't seem easy to me at the time.

But what are the odds that we could invade
this huge station filled with troopers and escape alive? I think the only thing we did that
Vader didn't expect was to rescue the
princess. And bring Ben to the Death Star to
get killed. . . .

No. I'd better not think about that right now.
Back to the point.

We headed for the Rebel base, knowing that
the Death Star was right behind us. It's on its
way here. That's not just Leia's hunch, because
a couple of scout ships have reported it moving
in. Unfortunately there's no way the moon can
be evacuated before the satellite arrives, so we
have no choice but to stand and fight.

Most of us, that is. Han decided that he's not
getting involved anymore. He said he's only in
this for the money, which he apparently owes
to some gangster back on Tatooine called
Jabba the Hutt. Leia made sure he got paid,
but I can tell she was even more hurt than I
was.

I tried to talk to him, too, to get him to see what I could: that the Rebellion was worth fighting for, and even dying for. The Empire had to be overthrown. Han just laughed and shook his head. He knew *I* was an idealist, he told me, but that just wasn't his style. He didn't really care *who* was in charge. He just had his job to do and a living to earn. He was taking the money and leaving. Chewie seemed to be less happy about the idea than Han, but both of them have made up their minds to go. Wookiees are loyal like that.

I have to admit I'm disappointed in Han. I really thought there was more to him than just plain old greed. No, I still think there is. The greed is just drowning out the rest of him. I don't understand it really, but I'm not in Han's shoes. Maybe if I'd grown up like he did, hand to mouth all the time, I'd value money more. I don't know Han's background — he doesn't talk much about it — but I'm pretty sure he's lived a dangerous and unsettled life. Maybe for him, bowing out now is the logical course of action. I'd like to believe so. I'd like even more to believe that he could fight for something more worthwhile than money, though.

He says we're all chumps for wanting to take on the Empire. That we don't stand a chance. That we're just throwing our lives away for nothing.

And maybe he's right — in part. We *could* all die in this fight. The Empire, after all, has a lot more resources than the Rebellion. And they've got their ultimate weapon, the Death Star. So, yes, it's going to be tough, and maybe we'll all die. But, even if we do, is it all for nothing, as Han claims?

I don't think so. I know exactly what I'm fighting for. I'm fighting for Ben, and Uncle Owen, and Aunt Beru, and all the people of Alderaan. For my parents. For those murdered Jawas, and for everyone else that the Imperials have ground underfoot, as if their lives were worth nothing. Because that's not true. Their lives were all worth living. And, if you ask me, it's worth fighting to make sure there aren't any more Alderaans, or Bens, or Jawas who are going to die just because the Empire says so.

So, I don't think that's nothing. I think it's a fight worth living for. And, if need be, dying for. I don't like the idea of dying, of course. Especially not now, when some of my dreams have started to come true. I'm out here at last, on a distant planet, under alien stars. I'm making a difference, fighting for a cause I believe in. And I think Leia really likes me.

Maybe I'm not the sort of guy who grows up to marry a princess. But I know now that I'm lucky enough to be friends with one. Despite her noble background, Leia doesn't have airs and graces. She's ready to fight and die with everyone else.

I even heard one of the doctors say she was tortured on the Death Star. She never breathed a word of that to us, nor did she let it slow her down. She's really remarkable, and I'm glad just to be her friend. And the nice thing is that she feels the same way about me.

It's really odd. Despite all of our differences, I feel like I've known her all my life. Or *should* have known her. Maybe it's the Force, or maybe just wishful thinking, but I've never felt as close to anyone as I do to Ben . . . Han . . . and Leia. Now Ben's dead, and Han's running while he can. It's just Leia and me against the Empire now.

But, somehow, those seem like pretty good odds to me.

It's not just the two of us, of course. There are lots of other Rebels, and one of them is Biggs!

I could hardly believe it when we ran into each other again. It was so great to see him. But such a complete shock. I mean, I knew he wanted to join the Rebellion, but I had no idea he'd succeeded and ended up here. It almost makes up for Han leaving.

Of course, Biggs was the one who was really surprised. He expected me to be back on Tatooine, still shooting womp rats and imagining space battles. Well, have I got some stories to tell him! After this battle, we are going to celebrate our reunion and catch up on each other's adventures. Big time! I can't believe I actually have my own stories to tell. Stories that won't put him to sleep.

Ah, this is great. Biggs and Luke — together again!

I had already volunteered for action, but I had to pass a flight simulator test before they'd let me fly one of their snub fighters. And Biggs was in charge of the test. I think he made it extra difficult, to help prepare me for the real battle. He ran a full combat simulation with high g forces. It was crazy! There were so many attackers coming at me, I couldn't possibly get them all.

So imagine how I felt when Biggs showed my test results to Commander Willard and Red Leader. Yeah, I was pretty nervous. Red Leader approached me and said I only got killed twice. Killed twice! That didn't sound so reassuring. But Red Leader explained that I had actually done well — considering Biggs had thrown an entire starfleet at me!

I would get a ship. And my wingman would be none other than Biggs. It felt so great to make the team, and to know that Biggs and I would be up there together.

I can't think of many people I'd rather have

fighting with me than Biggs. We go back so far together. When he left Tatooine for the Academy, I really started to feel like life was passing me by. Now we're back together — well, the galaxy had better watch out!

It was kind of funny when I introduced Biggs to Leia, though. He went all red-faced and stammering, and tried to say "Your Highness" without messing it up. I couldn't help grinning. I guess it's weird, meeting a princess for the first time. I was pretty nervous, too.

But, anyway, back to the point. Han's wrong about something else, too. There *is* a chance against the Death Star. It's not a very big chance, but it's the only one we've got. It seems that the station is virtually indestructible — except for one small weakness. The weapon it uses to destroy planets builds up a huge amount of heat that has to be forced out of the satellite. And there's only one vent for this. The technicians here have discovered that if this thermal exhaust port can be blocked, the heat generated will stay inside the Death Star and overload the systems in seconds.

Boom.

If we can seal the port. The problem is, it's very small, and it's located in an artificial canyon, guarded by guns. Most of the pilots who've volunteered to fight are convinced it is an impossible target. I'm not so sure. Okay, it's small, but not much smaller than a womp rat, and Biggs and I could shoot them from our T-16s without much trouble. A lot of the other pilots think I'm crazy, that it's a shot nobody could make. That's just defeatist talk. They've *got* to believe it's possible. Otherwise this moon is going to be rubble after the Death Star arrives.

I'm in Red Flight, along with Biggs. He's as convinced as I am that we can do this. I think some of our confidence is rubbing off on the rest of Red Flight, at least. We've got to be able to pull this off.

One more good thing — I'm not entirely alone in my X-wing. We need droids to help us pilot and run the ship, and I've been assigned Artoo. One of the techies commented that he's battered, and they have a few better models. But I won't go with anyone else. Artoo and I have been through a lot together, and this attack on the Death Star is going to be another joint venture.

It's almost time to take off. This might be my last entry. I could die in this raid. If so, then maybe this recording will survive, so someone one day might know how I felt about what's been happening.

May the Force be with us all.

I can't believe it's over! I'm absolutely exhausted and emotionally shattered. But it's over, and the Alliance is safe. Only, there have been more losses. . . .

These past couple of hours have been the most intense in my entire life — a whirlwind of action and emotions.

The Death Star had arrived at the Yavin system by the time we were ready to lift off. All our X-wings blasted off, and we headed into space. It's a good thing we didn't stop to think about it.

The Death Star wasn't very maneuverable, but it didn't really need to be. With its bulk, we could have shot at it for days on end and never hit anything vital, while it could destroy Yavin and all its moons in minutes.

Besides, they had the TIE fighters to keep us busy. They launched several waves of them, which came out to intercept us before we could reach the Death Star. We'd been expecting this, of course. My group, Red Flight, was assigned to run interference. Gold Flight, Y-wing fighters, were going to go for the exhaust port. They had stronger armaments and a better chance of hitting the target.

Leia had given me a kiss for luck before I'd taken off. Han, almost ready to leave, had called, "May the Force be with you." Not that he believed in it, but he obviously wanted to say something other than, "Good-bye, kid." Three-pio had told Artoo to come back in one piece. All our friends were thinking of us, even if they couldn't be up there with us.

And then the battle began.

I can't remember all the details because it was so hectic. TIE fighters were at us, cannons blazing. Artoo kept plotting and replotting courses, and watching the ship's systems closely. I just flew and fired. Biggs was close by me, and I know we saved each other's lives at least once during the fight. I'm not sure how many TIE fighters I got exactly. We were hit once, but it wasn't too bad, and Artoo had the problem under control pretty quickly.

Still, the Imperials were launching more and more TIE fighters. How many did the Death Star have aboard? There was no way of telling, but they seemed to have an endless supply of them! Of course, there were bound to be more

TIE fighters than X-wings, but I couldn't help wondering what we were up against. The only thing I knew for sure was this: the longer the battle lasted, the more likely we were to lose.

Gold Flight went in for the attack, while we covered them. Between the TIE fighters and the turret guns on the Death Star itself, it wasn't easy, but we did our best. Everyone was being rocked by explosions as the Y-wings went in. They switched on their targeting computers and entered the trench. The rest of us passed overhead, firing alternately at the TIE fighters and then at the guns below.

It was total chaos, explosions everywhere. But no matter how many we took out, there were always more. Gold Flight ran into trouble, too. The trench was long but narrow. One of the Gold Flight slammed into a wall and went down in flames. Another was hit by guns. But Gold Leader made it and let his torpedoes go.

And they missed. After all that, they missed.

They exploded harmlessly just about the same second the guns got Gold Leader.

And then it was just the remnants of Red Flight, as we whirled about as fast as we could, heading back into action again. We didn't have any option but to try again. The Reds weren't carrying very strong torpedoes — but theoretically, a couple of good shots from one of them could knock out the exhaust port. Theoretically.

Red Leader and two men went into the trench. Biggs, Wedge, and I provided their cover.

We dove for the trench together, trying to avoid the fire from the guns below. If we got low enough, they couldn't fire down. Of course, we had to virtually scrape paint off the Death Star to get that low, but Biggs and I had done worse back home on Tatooine. We'd taken some crazy risks as kids, and the experience was starting to pay off. It *was* just like blasting womp rats, even if the rats were fighting back.

I took another minor hit, and Artoo managed to reroute the systems. A stabilizer had broken loose, but the droid managed to get it operational again. Then the attack was on.

Flying low and firing like crazy, Biggs, Wedge, and I covered Red Leader. But we weren't good enough to stop everything. One of our ships went down, and then the second. Red leader fired his torpedoes, but once again he missed.

Maybe Han was right. Maybe this *was* impossible.

Red Leader went down in flames, and there were just the three of us left. And three enemy TIE fighters, including one that was being flown as if a demon piloted it. I was almost certain one was, and that his name was Darth Vader.

I could feel something odd, like a disturbance in the Force. It was like the disturbance I'd felt on the Death Star earlier, when Vader had struck down Ben. It was a feeling of great evil. I hadn't felt Ben die, but I had sensed this great, dark shadow in the Force. So I was pretty sure the pilot we were facing was Vader.

And I wanted to kill him.

Just not badly enough to jeopardize our mission. Right now, it was more important to stop the Death Star. I took a deep breath and made my decision.

"We're going in," I told Wedge and Biggs.

It didn't even occur to me until later that they were both senior to me, and they were the ones who should have been making that decision, not me. But they both accepted it as if they'd wanted me to take over.

Then we went in, Biggs and Wedge covering me. I had to really focus on my flying now. The trench was barely wider than my wing-tips, and any fluttering about could take us into one of the walls or towers.

And the stabilizer broke loose again.

Artoo was on it immediately, but for a second I was sure we were lost. I fought the controls to keep the ship steady, and somehow I succeeded. The shaking stopped, and all I had to worry about were the guns and the TIE fighters.

Biggs and Wedge got one of them, but the leader was on my tail now, maneuvering to get a clear shot at me. I had to concentrate on flying; I couldn't try to fire back. Then Wedge took a hit and had to pull out. The leader was coming in fast. Biggs tried to stop him, but it was no use.

There was another explosion.

It was Biggs.

As I watched his fighter burst into flames I went into complete shock. I realized that I no longer had any connection to Tatooine. First I lost Uncle Owen and Aunt Beru, then Ben, and now Biggs. My oldest and closest friend was gone.

Biggs and I had flown together on the razor's edge so many times, I guess I never realized that someone might actually get hurt — or even killed. How many times did we push our luck to the absolute limit? I desperately tried to focus on my flying and that fighter on my tail, but I couldn't keep the images out of my head.

Right before he left for the Academy, Biggs decided to build a T-16. From scratch. He said a true pilot should know every last detail about his ship and how it works. What better way to learn than to build the ship yourself? He wanted me to help, but I was wary of the whole idea. No way would he be able to build his own ship. I gave him a hand occasionally, but more often than not I just watched him in action. He was so consumed by his work that he sometimes didn't even know I was there.

Biggs was a good mechanic, handy with a torch and pliers. Good mechanics can repair and maintain ships. What Biggs didn't realize is that it takes a *great* mechanic to *build* a ship. He admitted that his finished product was a little rough around the edges, but insisted that he could fly it with anyone in any T-16. I couldn't help myself when he said this. I laughed out loud. Right in his face. Now, I know I didn't think much of the *Millennium Falcon* when I first saw her, but she turned out to be a fine ship. That's because Han deliberately made it look like a piece of junk. Biggs' ship, on the other hand, looked like a piece of junk because that's exactly what it was. This was no disguise, this ship was a true scrap heap.

Well, Biggs was less than pleased with my laughter. That was about as angry as I'd ever seen him. If we weren't such good friends, who knows what he would have done to me. He repeated his boast, and challenged me to fly with him. I wasn't exactly nervous that he would leave me in the dust in that thing, so I accepted his challenge. Thought I'd have a little fun with him.

What happened next was definitely not what I had in mind.

I thought we would go for a casual flight around the canyon. Since Biggs hadn't flown his creation yet, I thought that he'd want to test it out first. Kind of get a feel for the controls, see how sensitive its responses were.

But when Biggs blasted out of the hangar without a word, I realized how wrong I was. He was still angry and had something to prove.

"All right, Darklighter, you're on," I said out loud, even though he couldn't hear me.

The thrill of flight filled me as I chased him down.

It would have taken me thirty seconds to catch that T-16 if anyone other than Biggs was flying it. I could see it swaying and shaking like it was going to break up. Any other pilot would have been forced to slow down to get control. But not Biggs. He was so good, he was actually speeding up.

After about five minutes of chase, I finally caught him. Just as I pulled even with him and was about to commend him on his performance, I saw something small and metallic drop out of the bottom of the T-16. Two seconds later, something big fell out. Something very big. Before I could figure out that his bottom had given and the engine was gone, Biggs' ship was down.

It must have rolled end-over-end at least five times. When it finally stopped, the cloud of dust was so huge that I couldn't see anything. All I could do was yell his name over and over. But every time I cried "Biggs!" I was met with a deafening silence.

When the dust finally settled, I could see that he wasn't in the pilot's seat. Had he fallen out after the first tumble? Was he buried under the wreckage?

That's when I was tackled from behind.

I thought a krayt dragon had jumped me. But krayt dragons don't laugh. And they don't know my name is Luke. I turned and there was Biggs! And he was laughing! He was laughing so hard, he had tears in his eyes. But he was *fine*! He was looking at his wrecked T-16 and having a great time. I was amazed. How he could go through a crash like that, come out unharmed, and find the whole thing so funny I'll never know.

But then my mind was back in the present. I was in my X-wing and Biggs wouldn't be laughing after this crash. I reminded myself that I would have to mourn my friend later. Right now, I was in real trouble. The exhaust duct was coming up fast, but the TIE leader was coming up even faster.

I wasn't going to make it.

There were no other fighters out there, so I knew I was doomed. I could see the ship moving in behind me, and knew it was only a matter of seconds before it fastened onto me and opened fire. One shot raked my ship, and the link with Artoo died. I didn't know how badly he was injured, but he was out of the battle for now. The stabilizer could go again at any second, and we were almost at the target.

If I could hit it. I mean, I *knew* I was a good shot, but so were the others, and they'd failed. Maybe this is an impossible shot, I thought. Maybe this *is* different from shooting womp rats back home. I could feel my mind start reeling with panic, when suddenly I heard Ben's voice.

"Let go, Luke," I could hear him say. "Trust me. Reach out with your feelings."

And I knew immediately what he meant. The computer *couldn't* make the shot. It was too difficult for the machine. There was one way and only one way to do this.

I had to trust the Force.

I had to reach out with the Force and *feel* exactly the right time to fire the torpedo. Me, the novice Jedi, who's had about ten lessons. Who wasn't even sure he could feel the Force.

Ben wanted me to forget everything, disconnect the computer, and rely on my gut instincts. If I had any.

I *knew* it was the right thing to do.

I did as he told me and switched off my targeting computer. *That* caused some panic back at the base. They were monitoring me, of course, and asked me what was wrong. The feeling was that if the computer couldn't hit the target, there was no way I could.

And they were right. There was no way I could on my own.

But it wasn't just me. It was me, plus Ben, plus the Force.

Darth Vader was still after me, and closing fast. Without Artoo, I had so much to look out for, I could barely even track the TIE fighter approaching me. And his shots were getting closer.

I wouldn't make it to the target.

Then, suddenly, the TIE fighter was hit and spinning off helplessly into space. Over the communications I heard someone yell, "Whoopee!" and the *Millennium Falcon* flashed above me.

Han had come back! He'd changed his mind!

Maybe what we were fighting for had gotten to him. Maybe he liked me too much to let me die. Maybe he just wanted to annoy the princess by forcing her to thank him. At that moment I didn't care *what* his reasons were. He was back!

And laying down fire for me. He and Chewie covered me for the last part of the run.

Then I could see the target ahead of me. It looked so tiny, and I was coming up on it so fast. Was I just deluding myself? Was it an impossible shot after all? Was I nothing but a farm boy who shouldn't have been given an X-wing, let alone the responsibility of saving the Rebels?

I fought down my doubts. Ben believed in me; so did Leia, and so, even, did Han. Why else would he come back? They all believed in me, and I knew that I should believe in me, too.

I focused inward as I drew closer to the port, feeling for that gentle touch of the Force inside me. Reaching out to connect, and to know exactly the right second to fire.

And I *felt* it. The absolute, calm assurance that *now* was the time. My thumb pressed the button without any conscious thought at all.

Then I peeled away, up and out. The guns were still firing at us, but I didn't care. My torpedoes were on their way, and I *knew* it was working. The Force was with me.

Han and I headed directly back toward the moon at full acceleration. Neither of us wanted to be in the vicinity when the Death Star went up. I glanced around, but there was no sign at all of Vader's TIE fighter. Had he escaped somehow? Or was he dead? I didn't think he was. I was certain I'd feel a disturbance in the Force if such great evil were to perish. But I didn't have time to look for him.

Space behind us suddenly exploded with color.

The Death Star had powered up its planet-breaker just as my torpedoes hit their target.

The result was an explosion so huge, it blotted out everything. The shock wave sent my ship and the *Falcon* tumbling, but we managed to pull out of it.

The Death Star was gone, and Yavin was safe. The Rebel base was safe. Leia was safe.

I felt absolutely drained, completely wrung out.

"Come on, kid," Han called. And the *Falcon* nosed down to the moon below. I followed him in.

I heard Ben's voice again, this time with a promise. He sounded proud of me. "The Force will be with you, always."

I knew he was right. I *did* have a strong connection to the Force. Maybe I would become a true Jedi one day.

The first person to greet me when I landed was Leia. She threw her arms around me and kissed me, even though there were hundreds of people watching. I could feel myself blushing like crazy. Then Han and Chewie came over, grinning. Han claimed he only came back because he didn't want me to get all the credit, but I knew better. He came back because he'd discovered something better than money.

I made sure the flight crew took Artoo out carefully. Threepio hovered beside them nervously, but the mechanics assured us they could patch up Artoo without a problem. I really hope so. We've been through a lot together, and I've grown very fond of the little droid.

Leia says there's going to be a big celebration later, and advised me to shower and rest. I've just realized how hungry I am. A feast certainly sounds good. We've got a lot to celebrate. And to remember.

FOURTEENTH ENTRY

It wasn't a feast. Well, no, it *was* a feast. But that was afterward.

First there was the ceremony.

It turned out that Leia had managed to convince everyone that we were heroes — Han, Chewie, and myself, that is. As if all *she* did was stand around and watch us! But, apparently, everyone agreed that we were heroes, and we deserved medals. Han couldn't take his medal seriously, joking that it was cheaper than paying him a fee. I realized what an honor it was, though.

Then came the feast and speeches. It was amazing to see everyone treating the three of us with such respect. I think it may have gone to Han's head. He just lapped it up. I think he's enjoying not being a lone warrior for once.

He tried to blame his return on Chewie, but he doesn't fool me. That cold, cynical, cash-hungry exterior is just for show. Underneath it all, he's a decent human being. And, I think, a little embarrassed about it.

So now I've got a medal. Oh, and a repaired droid. Artoo was fixed up just fine, like the technicians promised. I'm glad, because the galaxy would seem a lot smaller if he weren't in it.

As with so many others that are gone.

I asked Leia about holding a memorial service for those who didn't make it. She told me I was the thirty-seventh person to request one. I guess I may be the most accurate shot among the Rebels, but I'm obviously not the fastest.

Everyone is relieved that the Rebel Alliance is still alive, and that the Death Star was destroyed. We can't stay here, of course. Grand Moff Tarkin must have reported where he was going, so the Empire's bound to have some forces out looking for us soon. The packing's begun, and our next base is being decided on right now by Leia and Admiral Dodonna and a few others. I was asked to sit in, too, but I declined. I really don't feel comfortable in there with all those officers. They've all been in the Rebellion so much longer than I have.

The past few days here have been some of the best and worst days of my life.

Worst, because I can't help thinking about all of those who didn't make it. Uncle Owen and

Aunt Beru . . . . Just a few days ago, I was complaining about having to work for them for another year. If I could bring them back, I'd go and serve that year without complaint. I really miss them.

Then there's Biggs. He and I grew up to-gether. We learned to fly T-16s at the same time, and we learned to fire blasters in the same canyon. He was like a brother to me, and I know he felt the same way about me. He was always there for me, right until he left for the Academy. Like he was there for me earlier to-day, when we faced the Death Star together. Biggs and Luke, together like always.

Only no more.

Yet, somehow, I'm not grieving as much as I'd expected. Because I can still *feel* him, some-how, through the Force. He's gone, but he's still a part of my life. In my memories, in my emotions, in the Force. If there's one thing that Ben has taught me, it's that death is not an ending. It's a change, the chance to move on to a new level. So Biggs has beaten me to it again. He's moved on to start something new, and left me behind to catch up later.

I'm truly glad for everything we've shared — from shooting womp rats to fighting together for the Alliance. We've had some very special times that will always be a part of me.

Biggs is one of the heroes of Yavin. And Leia

promised me that once this fight is over with the Empire, there will be a monument to the fallen, and that Biggs' name will be on it in a prominent place. He'd have liked that. He always wanted to be somebody, to make a difference, to me and to everyone else. He bought me time to finish off the Death Star. Rest peacefully, my friend.

And, above all, there's Ben Kenobi. I only really knew him for a couple of days. But no man I've ever met has impressed me more. His quiet dignity, his wisdom, his compassion. The way he saw something special in me, and encouraged me to live to my full potential. He was so *alive*, so real.

And . . . I'm not sure that he's dead. Oh, he's not alive as the rest of us are. But he's still around somehow. Of that I'm certain. He's spoken to me several times, and I know the voice is Ben's, not just wishful thinking or delusions. He only speaks when I absolutely need to hear something, and it's always to encourage me. If he was looking out for me while I was alive, he's not letting death deny him his job.

Although I've lost some very important people, I've gained some new friends, and a new cause. There's Artoo and Threepio. They might be droids, but they're friends, too. Oh, they can be real pains at times. Especially that

Threepio; he's a real earful. And they're both a bit too independent-minded for their own good sometimes. But they're irreplaceable.

And then there's Han and Chewie. A couple of disreputable smugglers, with an eye for fast profit. I know my uncle would have disapproved of them at first sight. But as stubborn as Uncle Owen was, he'd have realized that Han and Chewie are not your typical smugglers. And Aunt Beru would have definitely fallen for Han's free-spirited charm.

Han tells me I'm a fool to believe he's capable of anything good. But I know exactly what he's capable of. I know he can be trusted. Yeah, Chewie, too.

Finally, there's Leia — princess and Rebel. I can't help being impressed with her. Oh, not because she's a princess, oddly enough. But because of her courage, her conviction, and her absolute determination. When the Rebellion beats the Empire, she'll be one of the people to thank most. And she'll probably say she's done nothing. Because she's only doing what she thinks is right, and she's doing it with all of her heart.

How can you not admire a woman like that?

What a thrill. I will never in my life forget that fight. That I was finally able to actively do something. And summon a powerful ally — the

Force. It was the single most intense moment of my life. But along with this huge high, I'm feeling the lows and emptiness of loss. Ben and now Biggs . . . I never even got to catch up on things with Biggs. Which makes me sad.

But I guess that's the price one pays for having big dreams and going after them. For stretching to the limits of one's potential. If Biggs and I had stayed on the farm, we'd never need to catch up. We'd have all the time in the world. But maybe we'd have nothing meaningful to say.

There's lots for us to do now. The Empire's been given a bloody nose, but this won't stop it. The destruction of the Death Star is going to sound the signal for all the Rebels throughout the galaxy. They're going to be fired up by our victory and encouraged by our resistance. The Empire's going to discover lots of pockets of trouble in the days to come. But they're going to want to show everyone that the Rebellion can't possibly succeed. They're going to want to stamp us out, once and for all.

The immediate future is clear — the Empire is going to strike back at the Rebellion. So, we'll have to run and fight and run again. And we'll gather strength. Tyranny can't win forever. One day, the Emperor is going to be held responsible for his crimes. Darth Vader, too.

It's going to be pretty hectic for a while. But I'm certain we'll win — in the end. I don't know how long this will take. Or how many lives will be turned upside down, like mine was. But I know Ben was right. The Force *is* with us.

The fight for justice has begun. And I'm ready for it.

ENTER THE STAR WARS® INTERGALACTIC CONTEST!

Win a Poster that Really Glows in the Dark!

500 winners! *Purchase required.*

For a chance to win a Star Wars galaxy poster, buy all three Star Wars Journals and answer the essay question below.

Official Rules: 1. To enter, complete this official entry form or hand print your name, address, birthdate, and telephone number on a 3" x 5" card, answer essay question on separate piece of paper in 100 words or less, and mail together with register receipt(s) verifying the purchase of all three books (*The Fight For Justice* by Luke Skywalker, *Hero For Hire* by Han Solo, and *Captive to Evil* by Princess Leia Organa) to: Star Wars Galaxy Poster Contest, c/o Scholastic Inc., P. O. Box 7500, Jefferson City, MO 65102. Enter as often as you wish, one entry to an envelope. All entries must be postmarked by 8/15/98. Partially completed entries or mechanically reproduced entries will not be accepted. Sponsors assume no responsibility for lost, misdirected, damaged, stolen, postage-due, illegible or late entries. All entries become the property of the sponsor and will not be returned. 2. Contest open to residents of the USA (except residents of Vermont and North Dakota) no older than 15 as of 8/15/98, except employees of Scholastic Inc., its respective affiliates, subsidiaries, advertising, promotion, and fulfillment agencies, and the immediate families of each. Contest is void where prohibited by law. 3. Winners will be judged by Scholastic Inc., whose decisions are final, based on their answer to the subjective question. 500 winners will be chosen. Only one prize per winner. All prizes will be awarded before 10/30/98, depending on the number of entries received. Except where prohibited by accepting the prize, winner consents to the use of his/her name, age, entry, and/or likeness by sponsors for publicity purposes without further compensation. 4. Prize: A Star Wars galaxy glow-in-the-dark door poster. (Est. retail value of each prize: $4.00). Winners and their legal guardians will be required to sign and return an affidavit of eligibility and liability release. 5. Prize is nontransferable, not returnable, and cannot be sold or redeemed for cash. No substitutions allowed. Taxes on prize are the responsibility of the winner. By accepting the prize, winner agrees that Scholastic Inc. and its respective officers, directors, agents, and employees will have no liability or responsibility for injuries, losses, or damages of any kind resulting from the acceptance, possession, or use of any prize and they will be held harmless against any claims of liability arising directly or indirectly from the prizes awarded. 6. For a list of winners, please send a self-addressed, stamped envelope (residents of RI and VT need not send stamped envelope) to Star Wars Galaxy Poster WINNERS, c/o Scholastic Inc., P. O. Box 7500, Jefferson City, MO 65102 after 8/22/98.

ESSAY QUESTION (100 words or less):
What would have happened to Luke Skywalker, Han Solo, Princess Leia Organa, and the Rebellion if Darth Vader had never existed?

☐ BOY ☐ GIRL

Name _____

Address _____ (Please print clearly in ink)

City _____ State _____ Zip Code _____

( ) _____
Telephone Number

Birthday: Mo./Day/Yr. _____

Mail essay and register receipts verifying the purchase of all three Star Wars Journal titles to:
Star Wars Galaxy Poster Contest, c/o Scholastic Inc., P.O. Box 7500, Jefferson City, MO 65102.